—————— **SPY CLUB BOOK FOUR** ——————

MYSTERY AT THE SMALLHOLDING

BOBBEE MELLOR

Grosvenor House
Publishing Limited

This book is published by
Grosvenor House Publishing Ltd
Link House
140 The Broadway, Tolworth, Surrey, KT6 7HT.
www.grosvenorhousepublishing.co.uk

This book is a work of fiction. Any resemblance to
people or events, past or present, is purely coincidental.

A CIP record for this book
is available from the British Library

ISBN 978-1-83615-008-4

ACKNOWLEDGMENT

Grateful thanks to my friend and one-time colleague, Liz Drage, who has helped and encouraged me from the moment the Spy Club stories were first thought of.

CHAPTER ONE

It was the beginning of April and in the Valley Villages spring was considered to have finally arrived. After a mild Christmas and New Year, winter had set in with a vengeance, complete with heavy snow, ice and bitter winds. As far as possible people had stayed indoors. The animals, too, had tended not to venture out much and most of the members of Jake's Spy Club had seen little of each other.

Jake and his housemates, Libby, Ginny and Wesley, Siamese cats who lived in Lower Barton with Ma and Pa Dawson, had seen a lot of their neighbour, Ginny's boyfriend, Sherpa. He spent as much time in their home as he did in his own! However, they hadn't seen much of the other family Spy Club members, neither Ma's sister, Mary (known as Mad Mary to most people!) nor Claire, Ma and Pa's daughter, wanting to risk driving even a mile or two in the snow and ice, if they could avoid it.

The cats had missed seeing Jake's older brother, Max, and the two dogs, Brian and Tarran, and, in the worst of the weather, had worried about Mangy Tom, a stray who wandered the villages. Sherpa had assured them that Tom was well able to take care of himself, but it was still a worry.

As soon as April brought milder weather, Mad Mary took the opportunity to drive over one Wednesday, bringing Max and Tarran with her. When they arrived, Ma immediately put the kettle on – her favourite occupation according to Toby, the lively Jack Russell who lived on The Green – and she and Mad Mary settled at the kitchen table and began to chat.

The two animals joined Jake and the others by the kitchen window.

"We've got some news!" said Tarran, excitedly.

The four cats pricked up their ears. "Another case?" asked Jake, his interest caught.

Jake's Spy Club, a group of cats and dogs from the Valley Villages, had come into being the previous summer and had been instrumental in catching two nasty young burglars. Since then, they had solved two more crimes and Jake was ever watchful for a new 'case'. In spite of the difficulties and dangers they had encountered, he enjoyed the thrill of the chase. This time, however, his enthusiasm was immediately squashed by Max.

"It's neither a case nor particularly newsworthy," he said, looking at Tarran in such a way that the young dog, who was in awe of Max, subsided and said no more.

"Well, go on," said Wesley. "Whether it's a case or newsworthy or not you can't just leave it there."

Max looked at the four cats and then at Tarran. In spite of his manner, he was really quite fond of the young dog, a one-time stray adopted by Mad Mary the previous summer.

"Go on, you might as well tell them."

Tarran needed no further urging. "Mad Mary's taking in liveries. We've got a horse living with us. She said it would bring in some money." Mad Mary and the animals lived on a smallholding on the edge of Braybury, one of the villages next to Lower Barton.

2

Jake frowned. "Is Mad Mary short of money?"

Max shook his head. "She's not poor but she wants to replace the Land Rover which will be expensive."

Mad Mary's old Land Rover was well known around the villages, its rattles and clanks announcing Mad Mary's arrival a good minute in advance of her actual appearance. Everyone had been expecting it to give up the ghost for the last two years and it seemed now as if even Mad Mary had given up on it.

Tarran continued, "Two men brought a brown mare over last Friday. They are paying Mad Mary quite a lot to rent a stable and a field. She doesn't have to do anything with the horse. The men come over every day to see to her."

"What's she like?" asked Libby. "Have you spoken to her much?"

"Not spoken to her at all," replied Max, in a disinterested voice. He obviously disapproved of Mad Mary's new enterprise.

"We can't understand her," interrupted Tarran. "And anyway, she seems quite bad tempered. She ranted at us in some strange language."

"I keep telling you, she's French," said Max, "and she can't speak any English."

"Must make conversation a bit difficult," grinned Wesley. "What's a French horse doing over here anyway?"

"Lots of horses in this country are from abroad," said Max, in a rather superior tone of voice, which made Wesley feel rather stupid. He made a face at Max when the know-it-all cat wasn't looking, which earned him a frown from Libby.

"I doubt if we'll have much to do with her to be honest," continued Max. "The two men who own her don't seem to want anyone bothering her, which suits me."

The topic of Mad Mary's new livery seemed to have been exhausted but, before they could move onto another topic, the cat flap rattled and Sherpa appeared in the kitchen, moving across to join the other animals by the window and rubbing heads with Ginny before sitting down beside her.

Ma looked across at him and smiled. She and Pa had got used to always seeing him settled with their cats.

"That cat spends so much time here," she said to her sister, "that Arthur's beginning to wonder if he still has a cat."

Then she and Mad Mary turned back to their chat and forgot the animals.

Jake turned to Sherpa. "What's the weather like?"

All the animals looked at Jake as if he was mad.

"What's the weather got to do with anything?" Sherpa demanded.

The others looked at Jake wondering what he would say.

Jake laughed. "I was just thinking that, if the weather is still mild, we could arrange a get together. We haven't seen most of the club since Christmas."

The animals looked at each other, their eyes sparkling with anticipation.

"Not a bad idea, little brother," said Max. "After all, we don't want the club falling apart before a new case comes along!"

he added, jokingly, much to everyone's surprise. Max was not given to making jokes.

Everyone laughed and then Tarran said, "You'll have to make sure it's going to be held when Max and I are here. And Brian, too."

Libby nodded. "We'll have to keep an ear open for Ma making arrangements with Claire and Mad Mary. And we need to get Tom to take messages to the others." She turned to look at Sherpa. "Have you seen him at all?"

Sherpa nodded. "He's been about but, when the weather was really bad, he holed up at Sooty and Patch's. Mr McMurty seems to be used to him coming and going and just lets him stay when he wants." He paused and then added, "I'll go and find him when we know when we're meeting. Between us we can let all the others know."

As occasionally happened, Fate took a hand to help the animals out. The phone rang and when Ma answered it, it was obvious that it was Claire on the other end. Ma listened for a moment and then said, "Oh. Well, come over on Friday and spend the day with us. I'll ask Mary to come as well. Okay, see you then."

The animals had stopped talking and were listening carefully to Ma's conversations – first with her daughter on the phone and then with Mad Mary.

Ma put the phone down and turned to her sister. Before she could say anything, Pa came into the kitchen. He had been reading the morning paper in the snug, which is what they called the small cosy sitting room where they had their television. Ma said to them both, "Simon's got to go to London for a couple of days – something to do with work – so

Claire's coming over for the day on Friday." She looked at Mad Mary. "Will you join us?"

Mad Mary thought for a minute or so and then said, "I've got a delivery at ten, but I can come over after that. Do you want me to leave the animals at home? It gets a bit crowded with all of them here?"

The cats had a slight moment of panic and then Pa rescued them. "Bring them over. You'll only have to leave early to see to them if you don't. And, thanks to Ma's free and easy manner, all the cats and dogs in the area congregate here."

Pa looked at the group sitting by the kitchen window and winked at them. They were amused by how cleverly Pa had made it seem as if Ma was responsible for so many animals regularly appearing at the Dawsons'. They knew he had said it so that the club could meet up and they were grateful to him. Ma and Mad Mary would have been amused and completely disbelieving if told that the animals were in fact a team who worked together to solve crimes. If told that Pa was considered to be an honorary, and very active, member of the team, they would be completely dumbfounded.

During their second case Pa had come to realise, quite reluctantly, that the animals were working together and were adept at planning and organisation. And, in spite of a slight communication problem - they could understand him, but he couldn't understand them - they had forged a successful working relationship. It had turned out to be very useful having Pa as an ally!

Jake nodded slightly at Pa, who knew he was the leader of the group and that this was his way of saying 'thank you'. Then Jake turned to Sherpa.

6

"Can you and Tom arrange for the others to come over in the early afternoon. We'll meet under the apple tree. There's enough greenery now to hide some of the cats, so that Ma doesn't wonder why so many are invading her garden!"

Sherpa nodded. "Better be off then." He nudged Ginny affectionately and said, "See you Girl,", before disappearing out of the cat flap.

Pa smiled to himself as he watched Sherpa go. Something was being arranged. He turned to Ma and said casually, "Any tea left in the pot?"

Ma poured him a mug of tea and he sat down to chat with the two women while the animals lazed by the window.

CHAPTER TWO

The rest of Wednesday and Thursday passed uneventfully. The weather continued to be mild, so Jake and the others took the chance to wander around outside, noting the signs of spring around and about. Eventually they settled under the apple tree.

They were there on Thursday afternoon when Beelzebub, Sally, the vicar's cat, and his friend, Leo, called to see them. Leo and his owner, Marcus, lived in a cottage next to the vicarage. Just before Christmas Marcus had been kidnapped by three men trying to get back the evidence he had found, showing they were committing fraud. Thanks to Spy Club, with more than a little help from Pa, all had ended happily.

Beelzebub and Leo settled down with the other cats and were told about the Spy Club meeting the following day. Then Wesley asked hopefully, "Any progress with Sally and Marcus?"

Thanks to a comment made by Ma, everyone had been alerted to a certain warmth in Sally's manner to Marcus and the whole village, humans and animals, had been secretly watching the two to see if anything developed. So far, they had been disappointed.

Beelzebub looked at Leo and then said to the others, "He's taking her out to dinner in Littlebury on Saturday night."

"He said it's the first chance he's had to thank her for looking after him when he came out of hospital, because of the weather," added Leo.

Beelzebub sighed. "I think Ma's right. Sally likes Marcus a lot, but Marcus is so hard to read."

Leo leapt to defend his owner. "Don't forget he's already been hurt once." He was referring to Marcus's wife, who had died before Marcus and Leo came to the village. "He's just very wary now."

Libby said firmly, "Well, we'll just have to be patient and wait and see." Then she smiled and added, "And keep hoping."

The rest of the cats laughed. They all wanted Sally to be happy, she was such a lovely person. Then Beelzebub seemed to remember something. "By the way, I overheard Sally talking on the phone yesterday. The people who've bought the house on The Green are moving in tomorrow."

They all knew which house he was talking about. One of Marcus's kidnappers had rented it for a short time and Sherpa and Leo had had a rather unnerving experience in the house, while the Spy Club investigation had been going on.

"Any idea who's moving in?" asked Jake.

"A retired couple. They had a shop in London for a long time, but I think they originally came from Jamaica." Beelzebub was obviously good at eavesdropping! "She's called Betty and he's called George. Wilson. They're moving in tomorrow and Sally's invited them to church on Sunday so that they can get to know the villagers."

Wesley grinned. "What's a bet Ma goes to church on Sunday? I'm sure she'll have heard about them moving in."

At that moment Sherpa appeared through the gap in the hedge, used by the cats as a gateway between the two gardens.

He joined the group of cats and they brought him up to date on the state of Sally's friendship with Marcus and the people moving into the house on The Green.

"We'll have to get Toby to give them the once over," he grinned. Toby lived two doors down from the house in question.

By this time the cats had begun to notice a distinct chill in the air and so, with promises to be at the meeting the following day and to let Toby know about it, Beelzebub and Leo returned home. The others went down to the house and settled on the windowsill in the warmth of the kitchen.

Ma and Pa were in the kitchen preparing their evening meal and glanced at the cats as they came in, but hardly even registered that Sherpa was with them, they were so used to seeing him there.

"I'll have to see if Mary wants to come to church with us on Sunday," said Ma casually. "We've none of us been very often over the past weeks."

Wesley looked triumphantly round at the others, who couldn't help but smile. They could read Ma like a book!

Pa was not taken in either and said, equally casually, "I hear the new people are moving into the house on The Green tomorrow and Sally's invited them to church on Sunday."

Ma, completely unaware that Pa was gently making fun of her, said, "Yes, I know. I thought that it might be a good opportunity to meet them and welcome them to the village."

Pa smiled. "Oh, what a good idea." He looked at the cats and, when Ma couldn't see, he winked at them. Ma, still unaware that both Pa and the cats were getting a great deal of amusement from her attempt to sound no more than casually interested in the newcomers, added, "I think I might see if they'd like to come for coffee some time next week."

"That'll be nice," agreed Pa, wondering how long it would be before Ma had found out every detail of their lives. "But won't they be busy unpacking and sorting themselves out?"

"Perhaps," agreed Ma, "but I think I should ask. They can always say they're too busy."

Pa nodded. "Of course." Then he started carrying things through to the dining room.

Once Ma and Pa had settled in the dining room, the animals took the opportunity to discuss the newcomers' possible visit. To be truthful the cats were just as eager to see the new couple and find out all about them as Ma was!

"I wonder if we'll get to see them," said Libby. "Ma might take them into the sitting room and shut us in here."

"Then we'll have to make it clear that we want to join them," said Wesley in a determined voice.

The others laughed at his manner, but Sherpa said, "Let me know when they're coming and I'll make sure I'm here."

Libby looked at Sherpa and said severely, "Doesn't Arthur mind that he hardly ever sees you?"

Sherpa shook his head. "We have an agreement. He doesn't bother me and I don't scrag the furniture."

The others laughed at Sherpa's cheek but Libby, returning to the subject of the newcomers, was determined not to let them get too excited, and said warningly, "The newcomers might not even come."

Wesley looked at her with a 'poor Libby' expression on his face. "Oh Libs, do you really not know Ma better than that?"

At this even Libby had to laugh. They all knew that, when Ma set her mind to something, she usually got what she wanted.

Jake looked at them all and said, "Anyway, I don't know why you're all getting so worked up about a couple of newcomers to the village. I can't imagine they'll have anything to say that will interest us."

The others nodded, tending to agree with him.

Which was a shame as at least one topic of conversation would be of great interest to them if only they had known it. As it was, they didn't realise the relevance until much later.

CHAPTER THREE

Claire arrived quite early on Friday morning. Brian and the cats were happy to see each other again and disappeared up the garden to the apple tree. The cats brought Brian up to date with their news and he told them about his meetings with Jasper, his Golden Retriever friend, who lived with two feline members of Spy Club, Sooty and Patch.

Just after half past ten the noisy Land Rover announced the arrival of Mad Mary with Max and Tarran, who immediately joined the group of animals under the apple tree. They were all excited at the prospect of getting the Spy Club members together again, even Max, who tended to think getting excited about things was beneath him!

By two o' clock everyone was there. Toby, who couldn't climb the wall, had come trotting up the drive and settled by Brian. He had become such a regular visitor that it didn't matter if Ma saw him. However, it was thought to be safer for the feline visitors to keep out of sight, so they hid amongst the bushes near the apple tree.

Sooty and Patch arrived first with Mangy Tom, and Sherpa turned up accompanied by Beelzebub and Leo. Lucy Locket had been unable to come which, as it happened, turned out to be a real shame.

There was a lot of chat to begin with as most of the animals had not seen each other for weeks and had a lot to catch up on. Jake sat back for a while and looked on as the group of animals brought each other up to date with their news. He had been responsible for bringing the group together in the first place and felt proud of how close the animals had become and how well they worked together. Each animal knew they could rely on any of the others in a tight spot. All of them expressed disappointment that there was no mission in the offing and declared themselves ready to act the moment their skills were needed.

Jake suddenly noticed Max sitting slightly apart from the others, an undecided expression on his face. He caught Jake looking at him and tried to look at ease. Jake sensed, however, that something was troubling Max and he moved to sit by him.

He looked questioningly at his older brother and said quietly, "Anything up?"

Max lowered his voice and said, "I'm not sure. I can't help feeling that there is something not right about this mare we've got at the smallholding, but I can't put my paw on why."

It was not like Max to be so indecisive. Jake sat quietly for a moment or two and then said, "Think carefully. You're not a fanciful cat so something must have stirred your subconscious."

Max, glad that Jake was taking him seriously, thought back over the last week or so. Then he started to mention the things he had thought of as odd.

"The mare doesn't like the men. She acts up when they're there and they are very rough with her. I don't think they are used to handling horses. They come over and feed her, but they don't groom her. She's covered in dust and straw." He paused and thought again. Then he continued. "Sometimes they come in a small horsebox and take her off somewhere. She always seems in a better mood when she comes back."

He looked at Jake and smiled weakly. "It sounds even more pathetic when it's said out loud."

But Jake had been thinking. He looked at Max and said, "I trust your judgement, we all do. How about mentioning it to the team since they're here?"

Max thought for a moment and then nodded. Jake stood up – it had somehow become a signal to the others that he wanted to speak to them.

They all stopped talking and looked at Jake curiously. Jake nodded towards Max and said, "Max may have a case for us." He then sat down and left Max to explain his concerns about the mare and the two men.

"Why don't you ask her if there's a problem?" said Patch.

"We can't, she's French and she can't speak English," replied Tarran, eager to have his part in the conversation. "And she's rather bad tempered too."

"It means we're a bit stumped," said Jake. "We don't know if there's anything to investigate or not. Has anyone any ideas?"

There was a short silence and then Mangy Tom said, "I'll have a word with Lucy Locket."

Jake looked at him in bewilderment. "What! Why? How will that help?"

"Lucy speaks French," Mangy Tom replied.

The other animals, stunned into silence, looked at him as if he'd said Lucy came from Mars.

"Say that again!" said Jake.

"Lucy Locket speaks French," Mangy Tom repeated, emphasising every word as if he was talking to some very slow animals. Then he grinned. He was enjoying the effect his words were having on the rest of the group.

"Her family lived in France for two years when she was younger and she learnt to speak French. She was fairly fluent, although she might be a bit rusty now – not much use for French in the villages. Still, I'm sure she'll be able to make herself understood."

He was clearly very pleased to have this vital piece of information and looked round at all the other animals, grinning widely.

Jake looked at the others and eventually said, "Well, that's something I didn't expect. It seems the members of this Club have even more skills than I imagined."

Then he turned to Tom again and asked, "How soon can you see her?"

Mangy Tom shook his head. "It'll have to be Sunday afternoon or evening. She's away with her family at the moment. That's why she couldn't come today. They're back sometime on Sunday. I'll hang around and catch her as soon as they get back."

Jake looked a bit frustrated. "We can't really do anything until Lucy talks to the mare."

"Susie. They call her Susie," said Tarran and, under his breath, Max muttered, "Stupid name for a horse, if you ask me!"

"Anyway, nothing's likely to happen in the meantime," said Libby, soothingly. "We'll just have to be patient." Then she turned to speak to Mangy Tom.

"Could you let Max and Tarran know when she's going to speak to the mare – to Susie? Then they can make sure they're there."

Mangy Tom winked. "Anything for you, Beautiful!"

Libby smiled. She was getting used to Tom's comments by now, although Wesley still got a lot of amusement out of the fact that Tom had taken a fancy to Libby. He opened his mouth to say something cheeky but, before he could say anything, Ginny put her paw down hard on his tail. He looked at her resentfully, but she just shook her head slightly. Wesley sighed, but kept his comment to himself, simply thinking that Ginny was getting very bossy lately.

"What about the rest of us?" asked Toby, anxious to be involved somehow. The others nodded. Jake shook his head regretfully.

"I really don't think there's anything for the rest of us to do."

"What if we ask about to see if anyone's lost a horse, in case she's been stolen?" suggested Sooty, determined to find *something* they could do.

Jake nodded. "Good idea, Sooty." He thought it would be helpful for them all to have something to keep them occupied while they waited to find out what, if anything, was going on.

Tom got up and stretched. "Anyway, good to see you all but I'm off now." He looked at Sooty and Patch and added, "I'll probably see you tonight."

They nodded and then Tom was over the wall and away. It was the signal for the meeting to break up. Beelzebub, Leo and Toby, living near each other, went off together and Sooty and Patch followed in Tom's pawprints and headed back to Garston.

The home animals made their way down to the house, the cats going through the cat flap and the dogs barking until Pa came and let them in. He and the three women were sitting in the snug talking and drinking tea.

With the women safely out of earshot, Pa looked at the animals and said, laughingly, "Had a good meeting?" Aware that, if there proved to be anything to Max's concerns about the mare, they would probably need Pa's help, the animals looked hard at him.

Pa knew that look!

"Oh, Lord," he said. "What am I in for now?"

The animals felt satisfied that Pa was aware of their possible need for his services. They walked over and settled by the kitchen window and Pa realised that, whatever was going on, nothing was required of him at that particular moment. He gave a sigh of relief and went back to the snug.

The animals quietly discussed what might be going on at the smallholding for a while, then settled down to relax. Before they left the topic, however, Jake said very seriously to Max and Tarran, "We don't know yet if this is something or nothing, but until we do take care. Stay together when you're by the stables."

"I agree," said Libby. "And stay with Mad Mary when she's outside as well."

Max and Tarran looked at each other and then Max said, "They're right. We need to be alert and on the watch for anything odd."

Then they all settled to have a snooze, although in the back of their minds was the situation at Mad Mary's place. Max was especially worried. Now that his concerns were out in the open, he was even more sure that there was something wrong at the smallholding.

The animals spent the rest of the day in the kitchen, which was warm and comfortable, chatting about village events and carefully avoiding any reference to Susie the mare.

After tea, Mad Mary and Claire went home, taking their animals with them. Sherpa left at the same time. He said nothing to the others, but he was planning to hang around The Green the following morning, hoping to catch sight of the newcomers and get some details to take back to the others. He was a cat who simply had to be in the know – preferably before anyone else!!

CHAPTER FOUR

Saturday morning was cooler than the previous days, with a misty rain. Jake and the others settled in the warmth of the kitchen. In spite of Sherpa's secrecy, they were well aware of what he was doing and were waiting in the dry for him to bring any information he managed to find out. They were sure he would not be able to keep it to himself and they were right.

Just before lunchtime the cat flap rattled and Sherpa appeared, closely followed by Toby. Fortunately, Ma and Pa were in the snug watching television. Although, truthfully, Ma was nearly as used to seeing Toby as she was to seeing Sherpa.

Sherpa settled down by Ginny and, after helping himself to a drink from the cats' water bowl, Toby sat down on the floor by the window.

Jake looked at the two of them and said, "Well, what have you found out?"

Sherpa grinned. "They've got a cat."

Ginny looked at him in amazement. "Is that all you found out?"

Sherpa gave her a little shove. "I just thought he might be a candidate for Spy Club."

Toby joined in. "The couple seem very nice. The woman stopped to pat me and have a chat, even though she was busy."

"Did you speak to the cat?" asked Wesley.

Sherpa and Toby nodded. "Just briefly," said Sherpa. "He's called William and he's black and white. He was in the front garden but then the man came and got him and took him indoors before we could find out anything else."

Toby, deciding that they had delivered all the information, stood up and said he'd better be going, before Ma caught him in her kitchen yet again.

"She wouldn't do anything if she did," said Wesley, grinning. "She'd tut and make some comment and then smile and go off to do something else."

Jake grinned. "Pa's training her well. He's making her think she's the reason all the animals come to the house."

The animals all laughed at Pa's inventiveness and then Toby disappeared through the cat flap and set off home.

Just as he left the phone rang but it was obviously answered in the hall. After a few minutes Ma and Pa came into the kitchen. Ma was looking very excited.

"It'll be a lot better if I go in person rather than phone," she was saying to Pa. "They might feel awkward with strangers." And she grabbed her coat and disappeared.

Pa looked at the animals.

"Apparently the new people in the village are having trouble with their electricity and Sally has an appointment. She's asked if we can give them some lunch." He grinned and added, "Someone's on Ma's side today!"

They all sat and waited for Ma to return, which she did about ten minutes later. Taking her coat off she started taking things out of the freezer.

"Can you lay the table in the dining room, please," she said to Pa, "and put the fire on? They'll be here in half an hour."

It was a measure of Ma's culinary skills that, by the time the new people, Mr and Mrs Wilson, arrived, an appetizing meal was nearly ready. Ma had told the Wilsons to come to the back door – Ma and Pa rarely used the front door – so the animals were able to meet the newcomers.

When the expected knock at the door came, Ma was busy at the stove, so Pa opened the door. He introduced himself and welcomed them in. The woman, Betty, a tall, motherly looking black woman, thanked them both in a warm lilting accent which showed her Jamaican background, but which was overlaid with pure London! George stood quietly then shook hands with Pa when Betty introduced him. He seemed a rather quiet, reserved man.

Betty suddenly noticed the animals settled by the window. "Oh, what beautiful cats! Are they Siamese?"

Ma nodded. "Well four of them are. The grey tabby belongs to our neighbour, but he spends as much time in this house as he does in his own."

Just then the cat flap rattled and a plaintive miaow could be heard outside.

Betty looked anxiously at George. "That sounds like William. I thought you'd shut him in. He must have slipped out when we weren't looking. You'll have to take him home again George."

Ma walked across and opened the kitchen door. Outside on the step sat a forlorn looking black and white cat.

"Let him stay," said Ma. "Our cats are very friendly. He'll be fine." She stood back and William walked rather uncertainly into the kitchen. Before anyone could do anything, Sherpa got up and walked across to the newcomer.

"Hi! I met you briefly earlier this morning. I'm Sherpa."

William nodded but didn't move. "Come on," urged Sherpa. "Come and meet the others." He walked across to where Jake and the rest of the cats were sitting, William following rather slowly.

Libby stood up and said, "Hello, William. I'm Libby. This is Jake – Ginny – and Wesley. Come and sit here."

William, feeling slightly more relaxed at this show of friendliness, went over and sat by Libby. Ma looked on in satisfaction.

"See, they'll be fine," she said, smiling at Betty and George. George seemed to be a little restless and Betty whispered to him, "You can find out what happened later."

Ma and Pa looked at them curiously. "Is there a problem?" asked Pa.

Betty looked at George and then at Ma and Pa. "George is a horse racing enthusiast. He's got his eye on a horse called Blue Diamond, which is racing today. I've told him he'll be able to see it on catch up when we get the electricity sorted."

George, suddenly becoming animated, said, "She's a locally trained horse. She's at the Oakland Racing Stables, about ten miles the other side of Littlebury. She's entered for the Embury Gold Cup in July and I'm sure she'll win. She didn't do very well in her last race, but I'm sure it was just an off day."

Ma and Pa were both rather amused by George's sudden animation. He was clearly not just an enthusiast but a fanatic! At least where this particular horse was concerned. Pa was not an enthusiast, but he enjoyed watching a bit of racing occasionally.

"What time is the race today?"

"Now don't encourage him," Betty said reproachfully. "He can find out later if she won this race."

Sensing someone also interested in racing, George said hopefully, "Two o' clock" and got a reproving look from Betty.

Regardless of having spent a busy half an hour hurriedly putting together a very appetising meal Ma, a tolerant and easy-going person, said calmly, "Lunch can wait until after the race. I'll make a pot of tea. Pa and George can take theirs in the snug while they watch the race and you and I can have a chat in the sitting room while we wait."

If she needed any thanks, the glowing look George gave her would have more than done the job. He immediately joined the ranks of men who though Ma was a wonderful woman!

Ma put the kettle on while Betty sat beside the cats on the wide window ledge. William jumped on her lap and made himself comfortable. When the tea was ready George and Pa took theirs off to the snug and Ma settled by the kitchen table, realising that Betty would be just as happy in the kitchen with the cats.

As they chatted the two women found they had a lot in common, not just a love of cats. Betty told Ma about their decision to come to Britain from Jamaica in the 1990s, about the fruit and vegetable shop in Surbiton, which had been very successful and kept them busy. She spoke of her son, Thomas and his wife, Matilda, who now ran the shop and their teenage grandchildren, Curtis and Jessica. As with Ma and Pa, family was very important to the Wilsons.

Ma told Betty about Claire and Simon and about their son, Peter, who was working on a ranch in Texas. He had gone there at the end of his travels after university and should have been home at the end of February. However, the rancher had asked if he would stay on for a bit longer and he had enthusiastically agreed.

Betty laughed when she told Ma about the way they had chosen the area they wanted to move to. "I'm sure George pointed me in the direction of these villages because they were near to the racecourse. And, of course, this Blue Diamond is stabled not too far away as well. He's followed her since she first started racing. I shall probably end up a racing widow."

The animals sat quietly, taking everything in. Libby said to William, "Your owner seems very nice. She and Ma are getting on well."

"Yes," said William. "It's been nice to find friends so quickly."

The two women were still chatting happily when Pa and George returned from the snug just after two. George looked rather glum and was saying, "I really can't understand it. She won her first four races easily. The last two have been a disaster."

Betty looked at George and said sympathetically, "Didn't she win?"

"She came seventh out of ten. I've never seen her race so badly."

Ma, trying to cheer George up said, "Well, maybe you were right and she's had a couple of off days. Maybe she's under the weather. When's she racing again?"

"End of April," George replied, and then seemed to pull himself together. "You're right. She'll do better next time."

Ma smiled and said, "Pa, can you take Betty and George through to the dining room?"

When the four humans were safely settled having their lunch, Libby said to William, "George seemed really disappointed. Does he own shares in this Blue Diamond or something?"

William grinned. "No, he doesn't but you would think that he did, wouldn't you? He's just taken a fancy to her. He was following another horse for years and then it retired from racing and he started to follow Blue Diamond. She's quite a nice horse. She's a bay with a zigzag blaze on her forehead and a white blob on her chest."

The animals looked at William in surprise. He seemed to know an awful lot about the horse. William saw them looking at him and laughed.

"Betty's not interested in racing so I keep George company when he watches."

"You ought to tell him about Susie," laughed Sherpa. "Maybe they could make a racehorse out of her."

William looked curious so the cats explained about the brown mare and Max's concerns which, of course, led on to talk of Spy Club.

By the time they'd finished telling William about the club's exploits, it was clear that, if asked, William would be a willing recruit.

"Next time we have a meeting we'll let you know," said Jake, "and you can come along and meet everyone."

By this time William had completely relaxed with the other cats and, when the humans came through from the dining room, all six cats were fast asleep in a heap together, lulled by the warmth of the kitchen.

After a final cup of tea, Betty and George, with many grateful thanks, took their leave – they had an electrician, arranged by Sally, coming to try and sort out their electricity.

Assuring Ma and Pa that they would see them at church the following day, Betty picked up William and they left, talking on their way back to The Green about how pleasant and friendly the Dawsons were.

Back at Ma and Pa's, Ma was saying the same thing about the Wilsons, as she and Pa cleared away the lunch dishes and washed up. Much the same was being said by the cats about William.

As it started to get dark Sherpa left to go home, (the weather making a night watching television with Arthur preferable to a night on the prowl!) and the Dawson household settled down for a peaceful evening.

CHAPTER FIVE

Only Ma, Mad Mary and Claire made their way to church together on Sunday morning, Pa having decided to stay home. Max and the two dogs had come over as well, as Ma had invited her sister and daughter to stay for Sunday lunch. Simon was still in London and would be there well into the next week.

Pa, after giving the animals a searching look – just to check he wouldn't be needed – went into the snug to read the Sunday papers. The cats settled on the kitchen window ledge, the weather still being cooler than it had been.

The three women came back from church well over an hour later than usual. They had been chatting to Betty and George and brought back some news which made the animals prick up their ears. Pa came into the kitchen when they arrived home but, before he could say anything, Ma almost pounced on him.

"Guess what happened last night?" Pa shook his head and Ma continued. "We were speaking to Betty and George and you know that horse you and George watched racing?"

Pa nodded wondering what was coming next.

"It's been stolen!" Ma was clearly thrilled to have such news to pass on.

Pa raised his eyebrows and said, "When did that happen?"

"On the way home from the races. They were delayed and didn't leave until it was getting dark. The horsebox was stopped on a lonely lane – there'd been a diversion sign up, so they had to go a different way. The jockey and the stable boy, who was driving, were made to get out at gunpoint and two men with hoods on drove the lorry away. It was found a few hours later, dumped in a layby. The horse had gone."

Pa was about to make a comment when he noticed the animals listening eagerly to Ma. What had she said to interest them? He had his suspicions that they were working on a case, but he couldn't see how it could connect to the theft of a racehorse miles away.

Ma, thinking that he was not particularly interested, went on to start getting dinner. While she was doing that Mad Mary and Claire claimed their dogs and took them for a walk.

The five cats, left to themselves, were about to discuss the news when the cat flap rattled and Sherpa appeared, obviously with something to tell. Jake got in first!!

"We already know. Blue Diamond has been stolen. Ma heard at church and told Pa when she got home."

Sherpa looked very disappointed not to be first with the news but continued, "Do you think it's the horse at Mad Mary's yard?"

Five cats looked at him as if he'd lost the plot, even Ginny, who said, "That horse has been at the smallholding for well over a week. Blue Diamond disappeared last night. Don't you think there might be something a bit off with your timing?"

Sherpa nodded. "Yeah, I suppose so. I didn't really think it through, did I? Shame though."

Mad Mary and Claire returned with the two dogs and eventually the four humans disappeared into the dining room for lunch. The animals sat and discussed the situation at the smallholding and the strange disappearance of the racehorse. Other than involving two horses, the animals couldn't see any connection and decided that, firstly they couldn't manage two investigations and, secondly, they wouldn't know how to look into Blue Diamond's disappearance anyway, especially as it was all happening too far away.

Jake said firmly, "We need to concentrate on our own mystery. Let's hope Mangy Tom manages to see Lucy tonight. Until she can speak to Susie there's not much we can do."

The others agreed and the group settled down to talk about what had been happening in the villages since the cold weather had gone. After lunch, Ma made a pot of tea and the humans went into the sitting room. Before leaving the kitchen, Pa opened the back door for the animals to go out if they wanted. The weather had perked up, so the animals made their way up the garden to the apple tree.

To their surprise, not long after they had settled down, Mangy Tom appeared on the back wall. Seeing the animals under the apple tree, he jumped down and strolled over to join them.

"Any news?" asked Jake eagerly.

Mangy Tom, looking very pleased with himself, nodded. The animals made room for him to sit down and he said, "I've seen Lucy – they got back just before lunch. She's happy to speak to the mare. We've arranged for me to take her to the smallholding late in the morning tomorrow. The two men should have gone by then."

He looked at Max and Tarran and said, "Will you be there?"

Both Max and Tarran nodded, Tarran very enthusiastically.

"Good!" said Mangy Tom, and then turned to Jake. "I'll try and get over in the afternoon to tell you what Lucy finds out, but I'll have to take her home afterwards. She seems to have absolutely no sense of direction. Goodness knows how she managed to find her way here at Christmas."

The cats laughed and Libby said, "She came with Fred!"

Mangy Tom nodded and then they heard Mad Mary and Claire calling their animals to go home. Mangy Tom left and Sherpa went with him, after rubbing his head against Ginny's and saying his familiar, "See you, Girl."

Once the visitors had left, the four cats went down to the kitchen and indicated to Ma that they were hungry. It was a little early for their tea, but Ma gave in and fed them.

While they were eating, Ma said something which made them prick up their ears, especially Jake, in whose head an idea started to form.

As she tidied the kitchen Ma said to Pa, "Are you sure you don't need the car tomorrow?"

Pa shook his head. "Got one or two things I want to do at home. How long will you be out?"

"I'll leave about nine, but I'm going to call and see Aunt Jessie while I'm out that way. I should be back by teatime. Will you be able to fix yourself some lunch?"

Pa nodded. It was clear that Ma was going to be out for the day. Jake turned to the other three, who had obviously had the same thought. With no Ma to worry about them, they could make their way over to Mad Mary's smallholding in time to be there when Lucy spoke to the mare.

It was a pity she was taking the car but, privately, Jake thought they would have had trouble explaining to Pa exactly where they wanted him to take them! Communication was always a problem for Pa and the cats but, generally, they managed, one way or another.

They all settled down for the night with a bubble of excitement. Even if it turned out that there was nothing wrong at the smallholding, the suggestion that there might be brought a little excitement to their lives after a long, rather boring, winter.

CHAPTER SIX

Fortunately, Monday morning was mild and dry and there was even a weak sun breaking through the clouds. After eating their breakfast, the cats sat waiting for Ma to leave. Eventually, just before nine o' clock, Ma, smartly dressed and carrying a handbag, gave Pa a kiss and left.

As soon as the cats heard the car pull out of the drive, they went to the cat flap. Jake looked pointedly at Pa, who stared back at him. Then the cats all disappeared one at a time out of the cat flap. Pa watched them race up the garden and over the garden wall. He realised they were going somewhere specific, but he had no idea where. He thought it likely to be some distance and that they would be away for a while, since they had waited for Ma to leave the house. He hoped they were not going into anything dangerous.

Once over the wall the cats set off at a steady pace. The smallholding was just over a mile away cross country as it was on the Lower Barton side of Braybury.

An hour or so later they reached the smallholding and crept round the edge to the stable yard, in order to avoid being seen by Mad Mary. As they neared the stables, they saw Max and Tarran lying by the small haybarn, and they sauntered casually across the yard to them. They took great pleasure in watching Max and Tarran's eyes open wide as they saw the four cats approaching.

"What are you lot doing here?" said Max, almost unable to believe his eyes.

Jake grinned. "Ma's gone out for the day, so we thought we could risk being away from home for a while. Pa won't panic."

Before any more could be said, two figures appeared at the edge of the field nearest to the stable block, and the animals walked across to meet them as they reached the stables. The mare, in the end stable, looked at them suspiciously and said something which didn't sound very friendly!

Tom looked at the four Dawson cats and said cheekily, "Couldn't bear to miss out, hey?"

Jake laughed but said, "Come on, we've got to get back before Ma does. She may get home earlier than she said she would." He turned to Lucy. "Thanks for this, Lucy. It's amazing that you're going to be able to talk to the mare. Otherwise we'd be really stumped."

Lucy smiled at them all. "No problem. It'll be nice to speak French again. And nice to be able to do something for Spy Club a bit more demanding than looking round Avebury for people and cars!" Lucy was aware that this was her chance to shine with the other members of the team and she was determined not to mess it up.

She went over and jumped onto a water butt to the left of the mare's stable door, so that she was on a level with Susie. She said something the others didn't understand and, after a rather startled look from Susie, she and the mare had a long conversation.

The other animals waited impatiently to find out what was being said. Eventually, Lucy turned to Jake and the others and said, after a pause, "She says she's a racehorse called Blue Diamond. She was stolen and brought here by the two men who come to the yard."

Jake looked at the mare and then at the other animals. This wasn't what he was expecting at all.

"She's mad ... or lying." said Libby.

Max looked at Jake and frowned, "She can't be Blue Diamond, can she?"

Jake turned to the rest of the animals and shrugged. Then he turned to Lucy and said, "Blue Diamond was only stolen on Saturday evening. Pa and George watched her race in the afternoon."

The animals looked at each other, confusion on every face. No-one was sure what to do next.

Libby eventually turned to Lucy and said, "Ask her how she was stolen and where from?"

Lucy and Susie had another conversation and then Lucy turned back to the waiting animals. "She was out being exercised and someone took her off in a horsebox and brought her here." Lucy paused and then said, in a rather hesitant tone of voice. "I know you say it's not possible, but I believe her."

Tarran, who had been sitting back quietly listening, suddenly spoke up. "Ask her if she was the one racing on Saturday."

Lucy spoke to Susie, who shook her head fiercely.

The others still could not believe what the mare was saying. It just seemed too far-fetched. Jake said firmly, "It was definitely Blue Diamond who raced on Saturday. George knows her well. He wouldn't be mistaken. And all the people at the racecourse."

"But she lost," said Wesley slowly. "Badly! Again! When she was expected to win easily."

Jake looked thoughtful and then said, "We need to speak to William. He might know something which will make sense of all this." He walked over to Susie's stable and said to Lucy, "Tell her we'll look into it. We'll find out what's going on."

Lucy relayed Jake's message and the mare looked down her nose at him. She said something to Lucy, who laughed. "She said she's not going to hold her breath, but it was nice to have someone to talk to."

Lucy jumped down from the water butt and said, "I'd better be getting home again. Send Mangy Tom if you want me to speak to her again." With that, to the surprise of the others, she set off in the direction of Upper Barton.

Libby turned to Jake. "We'd better be getting back as well. Ma will be anxious if she gets back and we're nowhere to be seen."

Mangy Tom laughed. "She's a bit obsessed if you ask me."

Libby looked at him severely, "It's only because she loves us."

Mangy Tom tried to look apologetic but didn't quite manage it. "Oh, I believe you. Anyway, I'd better catch Lucy up and make sure she gets home okay. She's got no sense of direction, that cat." And with that he set off in pursuit of the fast-disappearing cat, who was completely unaware that she was heading for Upper Barton and not Avebury!

Once they had disappeared from sight, now going in the right direction, Jake turned to Max and said, "You were right. There's something weird going on here. I'm just not sure what it is. Hopefully, Mad Mary will be over at our place with you soon and by then we should have talked to William."

Max nodded and then said, "What do you think Tarran and I should do in the meantime?"

It occurred to Jake that it was very unusual for his older brother to be asking him what to do. Usually, Max had all the answers. Or thought he did! But he took Max's question seriously.

"Keep an eye on the two men. If this mare is Blue Diamond, she's valuable and they don't seem to be taking very good care of her. She might be in danger. And watch Mad Mary."

Max nodded, then turned to Tarran. "I'll hang around the stables and eavesdrop, they're wary of you. You stay with Mad Mary and guard her."

Tarran nodded, prepared to take his job very seriously, but he seemed uneasy. However, before he had a chance to say anything, with a nod to Max and Tarran, Jake and the other three set off back the way they had come.

Max looked at Tarran, he had noticed his restlessness. "What's up?"

Tarran nodded towards the garden. "Mad Mary's in the vegetable garden and she's been looking this way. I think she might have seen Jake and the others."

Max looked across at the vegetable garden, where Mad Mary seemed absorbed in checking the progress of her produce. Max shook his head. "If she did see them, she doesn't seem bothered, or she'd be hightailing it into the house to phone Ma and tell her. She probably wasn't looking quite in this direction."

The two animals, after a brief look at the mare, then made their way over to the vegetable garden to wait while Mad Mary finished her inspection.

CHAPTER SEVEN

The cats made good time home and, since there was no sign of the car in the drive, Jake was preparing to go straight to William's. However, Libby stopped him. "We need to see Pa first, to show him that we're back. He was watching us go."

Jake nodded and the four cats went into the kitchen, where they found Pa making a late lunch for himself. He looked at them closely to try to work out what they wanted of him. However, it seemed that the answer this time was – nothing! They turned round and went out of the cat flap and Pa, becoming attuned to the way the cats thought, realised that they were simply letting him know they were back from wherever they'd been and he appreciated it.

Outside they found Sherpa just coming through the gap in the hedge, looking a little put out. "Where've you lot been? I've been looking for you all morning."

Jake explained and Sherpa was even more put out. "You might have called me before you went!"

Ginny went over and rubbed her head against his. "We were in a hurry, but we could have done with you there."

The other three nodded and Sherpa looked pacified. "Did you find anything out?"

Jake gave him a rundown of what the mare had said, leaving Sherpa looking puzzled. "I thought you said she was in a race on Saturday."

Jake shrugged. "I know, it's weird. We're going to see William to see if he can help. He knows more about racing than we do. Come along with us."

Sherpa nodded and followed the others down the drive and out of the gateway. The five cats headed towards The Green and then crossed over towards William's house.

As they neared the house, they heard growling and the sounds of a vicious fight coming from Toby's garden, two doors down. Looking in alarm at each other, they raced along the hedge and peered anxiously through Toby's front gate. On his front lawn they saw Toby locked in a fight to the death with a vicious looking empty lemonade bottle! Their anxious expressions turned to looks of amusement, as they watched Toby finishing off his savage opponent.

Suddenly he caught sight of his grinning friends watching his battle. He gave his opponent, now lying still and quiet on the floor, looking rather the worse for wear, a final bite with his sharp teeth, and then sauntered casually over to the group of cats waiting at his gate.

"Practising for Spy Club," he said airily.

The cats nodded and Wesley said, "Yes, of course. You never know when you might need to take down a murderous lemonade bottle."

Toby grinned, not at all embarrassed, then said eagerly, "What are you lot doing here anyway? Has something happened?"

They told him what had happened at the smallholding and Toby said regretfully, "I wish I'd known you were going; I would have come with you."

Jake nodded. "It was a last-minute decision to go but we'll let you know next time."

Sherpa said, pointedly, "They didn't even tell *me* they were going."

Libby looked at Toby and said, "Won't Mrs Whittacker worry if you disappear for hours on end?"

Toby looked very pleased with himself. "Ah well, I'm training her to get used to me being out of sight for hours."

"And how are you doing that?" asked Wesley, wondering if it would be of any help with them and Ma!

"Well, I've been hiding every so often, a little bit longer each time. I've got it up to nearly two hours."

The five cats burst out laughing. "Where do you hide?" asked Libby.

"Under the bed in the spare room," said Toby, clearly very pleased with his scheme. "But I make sure she sees me outside first, so that she thinks I'm out somewhere."

The cats laughed again at Toby's cheeky plan and then Jake remembered what they were there for. "We're going to see William. Come with us."

Toby didn't need asking twice and immediately joined the cats as they walked along to the next but one house. When they got there Libby said, "How do we let him know we're here?"

Before anyone could answer her Toby barked sharply twice and within a minute William appeared from the back of his house, looking to see who was calling him.

Toby and the five cats met him at the entrance and, before William had got over his surprise at seeing them there, Jake said, "We need to speak to you about Blue Diamond."

Whatever William had been expecting it wasn't that and he was completely taken aback. "What?"

Jake quickly explained about Susie's claim to be the stolen racehorse. "We don't know what to think. Blue Diamond was stolen after Susie came to the smallholding, but Lucy says she believes her."

William sat thinking for a while. Finally, he said slowly, "They might have used a ringer."

The others all looked at him in complete bewilderment. "What's a ringer?" asked Jake.

William explained that some unscrupulous people swapped good racehorses with not so good racehorses who looked the same.

The others all looked mystified until eventually Wesley said, "Why would they do that?"

William shrugged. "All sorts of reasons. All of them illegal."

"Sounds a bit complicated to me." Wesley continued. "And does that help us with working out if Susie is Blue Diamond or not?"

Jake had been thinking and now said, "We need to talk this over. Let's go back to the kitchen. It's warm there and we may need Pa." He looked at William and said, "Do you want to come along?"

William looked back at his house. He knew that Betty and George were both busy and wouldn't miss him for a while. He smiled and nodded. "If it's okay."

The six cats and Toby sped across The Green and up the lane to the Dawson's house. As they all crashed through the cat flap one at a time Pa, in the kitchen washing up his lunch dishes, looked at them, a feeling of relief showing in his eyes that they were back again so quickly this time. He would prefer them to be there when Ma got home!

He looked at William and raised his eyebrows. "Are you a member now, too? That didn't take long."

The cats settled on the window ledge, with Toby on the floor near them and Pa settled at the kitchen table with a cup of tea. However, before they could start discussing anything, Sherpa said, "Looks like Mangy Tom on the back wall."

The cats all looked and, sure enough, the stray was settled waiting for someone to come out.

"That was quick!" said Libby.

Sherpa grinned. "He's afraid of missing something."

To Pa's amazement the seven animals went straight back outside. Then he saw Mangy Tom jump down from the wall and understood. Knowing they'd come and get him if they needed him, he settled down to drink his tea in peace.

The animals met under the apple tree and Mangy Tom looked suspiciously at William, although he said nothing.

Jake, realising that Mangy Tom was not particularly happy to see the stranger there, introduced them. "This is William, he's just moved into the village. He knows stuff about racing." Mangy Tom said nothing and William looked rather uncomfortable. Jake continued, "William, this is Tom. He's a senior member of Spy Club. We couldn't do without him."

The other animals looked at Jake in admiration as Tom, noticeably preening himself a little, looked at William and nodded. Jake's flattery had worked, although it was no more than the truth.

They explained to Tom what William had told them about a ringer. Jake shook his head. "It all seems a bit complicated. Susie might just be a bit of a nutcase!"

"Someone needs to go to the racing stables and talk to the animals," said Sherpa, knowing as he said it that it was an impossible suggestion.

Jake looked at him in blank amazement. "Are you mad? It's at least fifteen miles from here and through towns and built-up areas. It would be far too dangerous."

Mangy Tom, who had nodded at Sherpa's comment, said casually, "I'll go."

Everyone turned and looked at him in surprise. Jake shook his head firmly. "Thanks for offering Tom but, like I said, it's too dangerous."

Tom smiled. "I know what I'm doing. I've been wandering this area for years. Fifteen miles won't be too much of a stretch, but it'll take me a few days to get there and back." Then he looked at Libby. "I'll need filling up before I start. Any chance of a meal?"

Libby got up rather unwillingly. "Can't we get Pa to take one of us over?" she said, realising as she said it, that it was a completely unrealistic suggestion. They had absolutely no doubt that Pa would happily drive the entire Spy Club anywhere they wanted to go. The problem came in trying to explain what they wanted. Once again Jake and the others had come up against the brick wall of communication problems. He was not happy letting Tom go off, but he knew the stray, an independent cat, would do whatever he wanted anyway. He nodded at Libby, "Go and see if Pa will give him some food." Then he turned to Tom. "Take care. Don't take any chances."

"No, Boss," grinned Tom cheekily and then he and Libby wandered down the garden to the house where, as luck would have it, they found Pa still in the kitchen. He looked at the two cats and realised that Libby had brought the stray to be fed.

As he put a bowl of food down, he noticed that Libby looked uneasy. She was prowling back and forth, as if she was worried about something. Pa looked up the garden – he was well aware that the animals were having a meeting about something. He wondered what they were planning. Libby's behaviour was making him feel rather concerned. He hoped they weren't planning anything dangerous. Then he too had a momentary thought about the problems of communication.

Having finished his food, Mangy Tom, for once remembering his manners, looked at Pa and nodded his thanks. Pa smiled wryly. "You're welcome. Whatever you lot are up to, take care."

He paused as he picked up the dish and added, "You know where I am if you need me." Then he disappeared into the kitchen.

Tom looked at Libby and said, "I'd better be off. The sooner I leave the sooner I'll be back."

Before he could leave, however, Jake came down the garden to join Tom and Libby. "Just take care, Tom. Remember, don't do anything rash."

"And watch the roads," added Libby. "They'll be busier than the ones round here."

Tom looked at the two cats he now considered to be friends. All his life he had been a loner, until his involvement with the animals of Spy Club, and suddenly a warm feeling came over him. No-one had ever been concerned about his safety before and he found that it was good to feel that they cared about him.

None of these thoughts showed on his face, however. That would have been taking sentimentality too far! Instead, he just grinned. "Don't expect me back before Wednesday or, probably, Thursday. Keep an eye on things here." And he disappeared down the drive and turned in the direction of Littlebury.

Jake and Libby looked at each other but said nothing. Jake shook his head and turned to go back and join the rest of the animals, Libby following behind. As they reached the apple tree, the others looked up at them questioningly.

"He's gone," said Jake.

Seeing the looks on Jake and Libby's faces, Sherpa said breezily, "Don't worry, Tom can look after himself. He'll be back."

Jake nodded, still not quite convinced that Tom's venture was a good idea.

"What do we do while we wait for him to get back?" asked Wesley, not keen on the thought of three days with nothing to do.

Jake pulled himself together. After all, the members of Spy Club were not unacquainted with danger! Libby looked at Jake and said, "We need to speak to everyone as soon as possible."

Jake nodded. "We need to call a meeting. This is definitely a case now. Tomorrow morning about ten, behind the wall. Toby, can you let Beelzebub and Leo know? Sherpa, can you see if Lucy will come, and speak to Sooty and Patch?" The two animals nodded and Jake continued, "When we decide what needs doing, we'll get a message to Max and Tarran."

"What about Brian?" said Wesley, who felt his friend was getting left out.

"I don't know how we can get him here," said Jake, regretfully.

Sherpa and Toby got up to go. Toby went down the drive, heading towards the vicarage. Before he left, Sherpa looked at Wesley and said kindly, "When I go to see Sooty and Patch I'll go along to Brian's and bring him up to date." Then, after rubbing his head against Ginny's, he went over the back wall.

William also got up. "I'd better be going now. Thank you for inviting me. I'll be seeing you sometime."

"Aren't you coming tomorrow morning?" said Libby, smiling encouragingly.

William looked pleased. "Can I?"

The four cats nodded and Wesley grinned. "Like it or not, you're one of us now, a member of Spy Club."

William smiled widely, "Great! See you tomorrow." And he went jauntily down the drive, thinking how friendly all the animals in his new village were.

CHAPTER EIGHT

When the four cats returned to the kitchen, Pa was nowhere to be seen. He had gone into the snug. They settled by the window again, discussing the situation with the mare until, eventually, they became drowsy and nodded off.

They were woken an hour or so later by the sound of the car pulling into the drive and, shortly after, Ma walked into the kitchen. Pa had also heard the car and came into the kitchen to meet her.

"Good day?" he asked.

She nodded. "Yes thanks, although he drove a hard bargain. It's being delivered next Monday. I had lunch with Aunt Jessie. She seems fine."

"Good," said Pa, looking at the cats who were clearly curious about Ma's shopping trip. He added casually, "It'll be handy to have two cars. I don't know why we didn't think about it years ago." Ma nodded.

So that was it. Ma had been to look at a car and had obviously bought it.

She went out of the kitchen and then reappeared ten minutes later, having changed out of her smart outfit and put on the comfortable clothes she wore around the house.

She went over to the phone, saying to Pa, "I'll just give Mary a ring and let her know I've bought it."

She keyed in Mad Mary's number and waited for the phone to be answered.

"Hallo, Mary, it's me. I got it ... yes, I know it was a long way to go to look at a car but it's perfect ... What? What do you mean, our cats were at your place this morning?"

She was looking at Pa as she said this and he was trying to look surprised and innocent at the same time, although he had realised now where the cats had gone when he saw them racing off in the morning.

Ma was listening carefully to what Mad Mary was saying. At last she said in a bewildered tone, "Well, I can't think why ... Okay, see you then. Bye."

She put the phone down and looked at the cats with a puzzled expression on her face. She turned to Pa and said, "Mary said the cats were over at the smallholding this morning."

Pa put on a suitably surprised expression and appeared to be thinking over what Ma had said. "Hmm. Well, I shouldn't make too much of it. You know the animals like to be together. It's probably not the first time they've been over there, just the first time Mary's seen them."

Ma frowned. "But it's such a long way."

Pa laughed. "Only a couple of miles – less cross country. You forget, they've still got wild instincts inside those pampered bodies."

Ma seemed to be thinking about what Pa had said. Then she gave a quick nod and started sorting out the tea. Her next comment made the animals look at each other with great satisfaction.

"Mary's coming over tomorrow morning. I'll see if Claire wants to come as well, since Simon's still in London."

Her words made Wesley grin from ear to ear. If Claire was coming, she would certainly bring Brian.

Pa nodded but, in spite of his casual manner, he was thinking hard. He had suspected that the animals were involved in something new. This latest news suggested to him that, whatever it was, it was centred on the smallholding. He would have to keep that in mind. He turned to help Ma prepare the tea, but he was rather distracted. Fortunately, Ma was thinking about her new car and didn't notice.

When tea was ready, Ma fed the cats and then she and Pa took their meal into the snug. Not something they usually did, but Pa said he wanted to watch the news. He made some excuse for this to Ma but, in reality, he had no idea what was going to be on the news. He just wanted to be able to think things over without the distraction of a conversation and it was hard to chat when you were watching a programme.

The cats settled down after their tea, glad that Pa had apparently managed to smooth over the fact that they'd been to the smallholding. Having Pa as a member of Spy Club (although he didn't know it!) was really proving to be very useful, in more ways than one!

It was quite dark when Sherpa appeared through the cat flap to report back. He had seen Lucy and, although she was willing to come to the meeting, she found travelling from village to village quite difficult. Before her involvement with Spy Club, she had tended to stay close to home and, as Mangy Tom had said, she had a very poor sense of direction! He had arranged with Lucy that he'd call at Avebury if they needed her. He had seen Sooty and Patch who said they would be at the meeting. He had also looked for Brian, but he was nowhere to be seen. Wesley told him gleefully that it was almost certain that Brian would be coming over with Claire and so would be at the meeting.

Sherpa, who liked to be in the thick of the action, said, "I'll go over to Braybury every day to check on things." Jake nodded, then said, "No need to go tomorrow. Mad Mary's coming over here in the morning and will probably bring Max and Tarran."

Libby had been looking out at the darkness outside and said, "I wonder how Tom is getting on. I hope he's okay."

The others nodded and Jake, especially, hoped Tom was as good as he thought he was!

While the cats were thinking about him and hoping he was okay, Tom was making good progress on his journey. He had travelled several miles and was planning to find somewhere to sleep for a while. He had reached a small wood but decided it was probably safer to keep near the houses.

As he skirted the wood, he suddenly heard a terrified squeal. He turned in the direction it had come from and cautiously followed the noise into the wood. As he got near to the sound, to his horror, he saw a young cat being attacked by a fox.

He stealthily made his way as close to the two animals as he could and wondered what he could do to help. The fox was much bigger than he was and the young cat was so terrified he wouldn't be any use. Where was Beelzebub and his party piece when you needed him? Then he thought, if he can do it, so can I! He flattened himself, crept as close to the fox as he dared and poised to spring. He landed perfectly in the centre of the surprised fox's back. Before the fox had a chance to do anything, Tom dug his claws in as hard as he could. The fox yelled in pain and dropped the young cat, who simply lay on the ground, paralysed with fear.

"Run!" yelled Tom. "For goodness' sake, run!"

The young cat, suddenly coming to his senses, gasped, "Thank you! Thank you!" and took to his heels, running as fast as he could until he reached the safety of his home, promising himself that he would never leave the protection of his garden again.

Meanwhile, Tom had been left wondering how he was going to get himself out of the situation he was in. He gave a last stab with his claws into the back of the angry fox, who was struggling in an attempt to dislodge the cat, and then leapt quickly off and scaled a tree before the fox had a chance to recover.

The fox snarled and turned to look up at Tom.

"You interfering busybody!"

"Sorry!" said Tom, not a bit sorry really. "Couldn't stand by and see you hurt a fellow cat."

The fox gave him a poisonous look and slunk off. Tom smiled and thought that, when he got home, he must thank Beelzebub for showing him that little trick. Very effective!

He was just about to climb down the tree, when the memory of the look the fox had given him made him pause. It occurred to him that the fox might possibly be lying in wait for him somewhere. He looked around and realised how dark it was in the wood, so he made himself comfortable and decided to wait until it started to get light before he continued his journey. He knew time was important and it would delay him quite a bit, but better than the fox getting him and him not reaching the racing stables at all.

CHAPTER NINE

Fortunately, Tuesday dawned dry and mild again. After breakfast the cats waited for Mad Mary and Claire to arrive, bringing Max and the two dogs. They were a little later than expected, so most of the team were already behind the wall waiting. Jake called them into the garden – Brian and Tarran would attract attention if they jumped the wall – and the visiting cats hid in the shrubbery while they waited for Toby to run round to the front entrance. With all the will in the world, his short legs wouldn't allow him to scale the wall!

Jake asked William to explain his idea about a 'ringer' and then told them about Tom's trek to the racing stables. Those who hadn't known about this were rather taken aback, like Jake, worrying about the distance. However, again Sherpa assured them that Tom was well able to take care of himself. He told them of his plan to check in at the smallholding every day and to fetch Lucy, if necessary.

Jake then told them that Max would eavesdrop whenever the men were at the stable, and Tarran would stay close to Mad Mary if she was at the stable block, just in case.

All the animals agreed that these were useful steps to take and that there was little more they could do for the time being. Jake turned to Max and asked, "Were the men at the stables this morning?"

Max nodded, "They were, but they took her off almost immediately in the horsebox. She looks a very scruffy animal, and she played up no end. One of the men, Charlie his name is, got kicked on the leg and said something I couldn't repeat."

Wesley, a wicked look in his eye said, "Go on, Max. Tell us what he said!"

He got a reproving look from Libby and Max said in a bored tone of voice, "I suppose you *will* grow up one of these days."

"Not if it means being as po-faced as you!" Wesley muttered under his breath. Fortunately, only Sherpa heard him and grinned at him behind Max's back!

Brian, who had apparently been deep in thought, suddenly said, "Where do they take her?"

It was obvious that no-one else had wondered about this. Everyone looked at Max and Tarran, who both shrugged.

Tarran said, "We should have thought about that and got Lucy to ask her."

Jake nodded. "We'll get her to ask next time she's at the smallholding. It might be important."

Beelzebub looked hard at Jake and said, "Do you think the mare is telling the truth? That she's this Blue Diamond racehorse?"

Jake looked at him and then at the others. "I really don't know. We could be investigating something when there's nothing to be investigated. In fact, she doesn't look like William described her. She's supposed to have a zigzag blaze on her nose."

William half stood up, nervous at speaking out in front of everyone. Libby smiled at him kindly. "Yes, William?"

"They can use dyes," he said hesitantly, "to hide things and to put them on."

Beelzebub spoke up again and asked the question in everyone's minds. "Why would they do it? Swop the horses and then steal the replacement?"

William shook his head. "I don't know. It's a pity we can't ask George. He knows a lot about what goes on in racing."

"Same problem we have with Pa," said Jake. "Communication."

"The problem we actually have," a grinning Wesley said cheekily, "is that we have absolutely no idea what we're investigating!"

The others looked at him and then suddenly Jake started to laugh.

"You know young Wesley, you're not far wrong there," he said, and all the animals laughed as well. "We just need to be ready for whatever crops up."

Beelzebub said thoughtfully, "It would help if we knew whether this mare is Blue Diamond or simply barmy!"

"If Blue Diamond has this distinctive white blaze," said Sooty, "and this mare at the smallholding is Blue Diamond, then they must have covered it up – dyed it, as William said." She turned to Max. "Would you be able to have a close look at the mare's nose, to see if there are any signs of white hairs?"

Max nodded. "Oh yes, I might be able to do that, but it wouldn't be any good. I wouldn't be able to tell any of you."

"Why not?" asked Libby, confused.

"Because the mare would bite my head off, that's why," said Max icily. "Blue Diamond or not, she's not the sweetest tempered creature."

He looked round at the others and then smiled amiably. "Anyway, I have no intention of making the attempt."

"Fair enough." Jake thought he probably wouldn't want to do it either. He looked around at the members of his team.

"We need to keep in touch. We have no idea what's going to happen, so we need to be on red alert. We need to be ready to act at a moment's notice, but we can't really do anything until we hear from Mangy Tom. Unless something happens in the meantime, of course."

The talk then became more general, everyone realising that any further talk of the mare would be pointless. The animals chatted for a while and then Wesley, suddenly thinking of something, said to Beelzebub and Leo, "How did Sally and Marcus's dinner out go?"

The rest of the animals immediately turned to hear the answer. Beelzebub looked at Leo and they both shrugged.

"Sally seemed quite happy when she got home," said Beelzebub. "She was humming, and she took ages to get ready to go out. She must have tried on every dress she owns before she finally chose one."

"What about Marcus?" Libby asked Leo.

Leo smiled. "Well, he was whistling when he was getting ready for bed. I haven't heard him do that for a while."

"Sounds promising," said Wesley, gleefully.

Beelzebub and Leo laughed. They had a good feeling about their two owners. As Libby had said before - time would tell.

Eventually the visiting animals left for home, careful not to be too noticeable. Sooty and Patch left to return to Garston, and Beelzebub and Leo went back to the vicarage. Even Toby went home, feeling he had stretched his time out of Mrs Whittacker's sight as long as he could. He and William went off together, chatting in a friendly way, as if they'd known each other for years!

As the weather was so pleasant, Jake and the others stayed under the apple tree, talking lazily about this and that. However, in spite of their best attempts, the situation at the smallholding was always at the back of their minds.

CHAPTER TEN

While the members of Spy Club had been having their meeting and then lounging in the garden, Mangy Tom had been making steady progress towards his destination. Just before midnight, tired and hungry, he arrived at the front entrance of the Oakland Racing Stables.

The gates were closed and padlocked, so he scrambled up the high wall and sat looking down into the yard. All seemed quiet, so he jumped down onto a patch of grass and looked round. All the stable doors were shut, although he could hear occasional movement inside one or two.

As he started to walk across the yard, a security light came on and he paused. He was just about to carry on when, almost out of nowhere, he was confronted by a very large, very unfriendly looking ginger cat.

"This is private property, mate. Get lost!" said the ginger cat menacingly.

Tom stood still and looked carefully at the fierce looking cat, trying to work out how difficult he might be to talk to.

Then he said, conversationally, "Do you know a horse called Blue Diamond?"

The ginger cat looked as if he had been about to take steps to remove Tom from the yard, but this comment stopped him in his tracks.

"What do you know about Blue Diamond?" he said, his eyes narrowed with suspicion.

Tom sat down and then said, in an offhand tone of voice, "I've got some information about her, if you're interested. But I need some information in return."

The ginger cat looked at Tom long and hard for several seconds. Then he seemed to come to a decision, apparently satisfied with that he saw.

"Come into the barn," he said abruptly, and turned and walked towards a large brick building to the side of the yard. Tom got up and followed him, sincerely hoping it wasn't a trick.

The ginger cat disappeared through a hole in the wall and Tom followed. Inside the barn he saw three other cats, two black and white and one a dirty grey colour. They had obviously been waiting for the ginger cat to report back. When they saw Tom they sprang up, coats bushed out.

"Stow it!" said the ginger cat and the three immediately subsided. It was clear who was the boss. He turned to Tom and said, "Introductions first. I'm Ginger – humans have no imagination! – this is Sam and Joe," pointing to the two black and white cats, "and Smoky."

The cats all nodded at Tom, who said jauntily, "Mangy Tom."

The four cats looked at him rather taken aback. Tom laughed. "It's because so many humans kept saying, 'who does that mangy tom belong to?' Well, I don't belong to anyone and I like it like that. Call me Tom."

Ginger nodded and then got down to business. "Now, what do you know about Blue Diamond?"

The eyes of the other three cats widened but, before they could say anything, Ginger turned to them and said, "Tom says he's got some information about her but wants us to give him some information in return." He looked at Tom and said firmly, "You first."

Aware that he was on their territory, Tom took a deep breath. "There's a horse being kept in a stable near us says she's Blue Diamond. She's been there nearly a fortnight, but we've only just found a cat who can speak French."

Sam looked amazed. "You know a cat who can speak French?"

Ginger looked at him impatiently and then turned back to Tom. "It can't be Blue Diamond. Blue only went missing on Saturday evening."

Tom nodded. "Is it possible that the horse who went missing on Saturday wasn't Blue Diamond?"

For a second Ginger's eyes opened wide at this. "What are you suggesting?" he asked Tom, frowning.

"We think Blue Diamond was swopped for another horse, so that she'd apparently go missing long after this horse was taken to the smallholding. That way, no-one would suspect that it was Blue Diamond. If so, they've covered her blaze and the white patch on her chest."

"A ringer," said Ginger, thoughtfully.

"We wondered if it was, if it could be done. Would the humans realise it was a different horse? William is the only one who knows anything about racing and horses and he wasn't sure."

Ginger was thinking hard, so Sam took the opportunity to speak to Tom. "Where is this smallholding and who's William?"

Tom smiled. "It's in Braybury, one of the Valley Villages on the other side of Littlebury.

Sam gawped. "That's fifteen miles from here. You've walked all that way? Why?"

Tom said, not without a touch of pride, "I belong to a gang of village cats and dogs. We solve crimes."

Even Ginger paid attention to this. "You do what?"

"We solve crimes. This is our fourth case. Two of our members live on the smallholding and they had a feeling that something wasn't right. William is a newcomer to the villages, but his owner is a keen follower of racing. That's how we started to suspect something was up."

Ginger seemed to come to a decision. "Thinking about it, it's possible you could be right. The only thing is, her groom and jockey would have to be in on it. There's no way they wouldn't realise it's a different horse."

"Is that possible, in this case?" asked Tom.

Joe's eyes opened wide. "I heard John say that he had paid his debts the other day. Maybe he's been paid to keep quiet."

Mangy Tom looked questioningly at Ginger, who nodded. "John's the stable boy who looks after Blue. He says all the right things to the bosses but, in reality, he's not really very committed to the job. He could easily be bribed."

"What about the jockey?" asked Tom, "and the people who train her?"

"Her trainer's been over in Ireland looking at some new horses. As far as the jockey's concerned, I would say no way. Steve's fond of Blue and would never do anything to hurt her."

"But?" said Tom, hearing a note of indecision in Ginger's tone.

"He had an accident just over two weeks ago. Broke his leg. There's a new jockey been riding her."

Ginger looked at his friends. "It could be done."

Mangy Tom had been thinking. "Do you think Steve's accident could have been arranged deliberately?"

Ginger nodded. "He was furious apparently. He was out alone exercising Blue and someone fired a gun over her head. She threw him and bolted. Back here, fortunately. The new jockey turned up the next day, offering his services. I never thought anything of it at the time, but now it seems rather coincidental."

"What are we going to do?" asked Smoky.

"Nothing!" said Tom, firmly. "Leave it to us. Now we know the truth we can sort something out. The villages are too far away from here for any toing and froing. It's taken me well over a day to get here and I'm worn out. I'd appreciate somewhere to sleep and a snack before I set off again."

Ginger nodded. "Sorry, forgetting my manners." And he led Tom across to an automatic feeder, where Tom ate his fill and then settled in a far corner of the barn to sleep, saying, "Wake me well before dawn please. I want to get out of the area before the roads get too busy."

The four cats left him to sleep and sat discussing the information they'd been given.

"We need to keep an eye on John and that Milligan guy," said Joe. Then he asked the same question Beelzebub had asked. "Why do it anyway? What's the point? Why not just take Blue Diamond in the first place? Why swop her for a ringer and then steal the ringer. It just doesn't make sense."

Ginger shrugged. "I suppose there must have been a point, but I can't imagine what it is. Explains why Blue did so badly in her last two races. It wasn't Blue."

When the stable yard came alive, just after dawn, everyone, except the four yard cats, was surprised when neither John the stable boy nor the replacement jockey arrived for work. When the angry yard manager tried to get hold of them, neither was answering his phone.

By this time Mangy Tom was well on his way back home, having filled up at the automatic feeder before leaving.

He said 'goodbye' to Sam, Joe and Smoky and then Ginger showed him a shortcut, which would take him round the edge of the town, shortening his journey by a couple of miles.

As they said goodbye Tom looked at Ginger and said, in a rather regretful tone, "It's a pity you're so far away. We could do with you in Spy Club."

"Spy Club?" laughed Ginger.

Tom laughed as well. "That's what Wesley called us. He's a cheeky monkey but a good member of the team. You never know, one day you might get to meet them all."

The two cats nodded at each other in a friendly way and then Tom set off, following the route Ginger had pointed out to him. Ginger watched him for a minute or two and then turned and made his way back to the racing yard.

CHAPTER ELEVEN

Mangy Tom made good time on his return journey, thanks partly to Ginger's shortcut. He had a largely uneventful journey, except for an incident near the small wood, which would prove to be extremely useful.

He had decided to go round the edge of the wood, just in case the angry fox was still lurking there, and was making his way down a path going along the back of a row of small gardens when he saw a cat sitting on the fence of one of the gardens. Not inclined to be drawn into wasting time chatting, he nodded briefly as he passed the cat and was pressing on when the cat stood up and said excitedly, "It's you. It is. It's you."

Tom stopped and looked back at the cat, who looked vaguely familiar.

"It's me," said the cat. "You saved me from the fox. I'm so glad to see you again, so that I can thank you properly."

Tom was about to say that he was glad to have been of help and then to press on with his journey, when it occurred to him that he might get a meal from the little cat. It was several hours since he had left the racing stables and he hadn't eaten since then.

He walked over to the young cat and said, "You're very welcome." Then he explained about his journey to and from the racing stables and asked if there was any chance of a snack. The little cat, who said his name was Bertie, was only too glad to help and told Tom to come into the house, his owners were out so he'd be quite safe.

Tom followed Bertie into the garden and then through a cat flap, into what looked like a utility room. Within seconds he was finishing up the food left in Bertie's dishes. While he had eaten Bertie had plied him with questions about his journey so, when he'd finished eating, he sat with Bertie and explained about Blue Diamond and the mare at the smallholding. Bertie was entranced.

"My owner, David, is a racing fan. I've heard of Blue Diamond. David and his friend were talking about her. I think someone wanted to buy her. Everyone thought she'd be sure to win the Embury Cup, but she lost her last two races and then she was stolen. Her owner must be very worried."

Tom looked closely at Bertie and said, "Who is her owner?"

Bertie, pleased to have the information that Tom wanted, said, "I don't know his name but he's a sheet."

Tom looked at Bertie and repeated, "He's a sheet?"

Bertie nodded. "He's from Saudi Arabia or somewhere like that but he lives in France a lot of the time. He's very rich. He comes over to the races in his own plane."

Tom finally managed to make sense of Bertie's comment and struggled not to laugh as he said, kindly, "I think you mean he's a sheik."

Bertie looked interested. "Do I? Anyway, he was coming over to see Blue Diamond racing at the end of April and then she was stolen, so I don't know if he'll still come."

Tom was looking at Bertie, his mind full of possibilities. He said, "I think you've just repaid me for saving you from the fox!"

Bertie looked rather confused. "I did? How did I do that?"

Tom shook his head, "Never mind. Anyway, I must get going." And he made his way out through the cat flap, followed by Bertie.

"Thanks for the food," he said, heading for the back fence. Before he jumped over, he turned and said, "Take care in the wood in future."

Bertie laughed rather nervously. "I will. Thank you again."

Tom set off once more, his conversation with Bertie running through his mind. He smiled in satisfaction. In spite of Jake's concerns, the journey had been well worth the effort. He would have a lot to report back to the members of Spy Club when he got home.

He considered finding somewhere to sleep for a while but, thanks to Ginger, he could be back home in a few hours if he kept going. He decided that he needed to get his information back to the team as soon as possible and so he pressed on. He was used to wandering about the countryside, day and night, and, unlike poor Lucy, had an excellent sense of direction. He skilfully retraced his steps and, just as it started to get dark, he reached the edge of the Valley Villages. Just under an hour later he was approaching the turning into the lane where the Dawsons lived.

As Tom was making his way along the lane to the Dawson's house, the four cats were finishing off their tea. Wesley, having polished off his food rather speedily, jumped onto the window ledge to gaze out of the window. Almost at once he saw a shadow moving in the garden. He peered hard and suddenly realised who it was.

"Tom's in the garden," he yelled, startling the other three cats, as well as Ma and Pa.

Jake rushed over to the window and saw Tom prowling round near the house. "He's right. Tom's back. Ginny, go and get Sherpa, quickly."

To Ma's amazement the cats raced out of the cat flap as if they were being chased by a pack of wolves. Pa was less startled than Ma, simply because he had been aware that they were up to something and, also, he'd seen the shadowy figure in the garden when Wesley yelled out.

He looked at Ma, shrugged and said, in an offhand tone of voice, "They're a bit skittish, enjoying being able get outside again."

Ma looked at him, then simply shook her head and went to wash the dishes.

When the cats got outside, they found that Tom had gone to wait under the apple tree. As they made their way up the garden, they met Ginny and Sherpa coming through the gap in the hedge. They all raced up the garden to greet the wanderer and the next few minutes were filled with five cats all asking Tom questions at the same time. He grinned, but said nothing and, eventually, the cats stopped talking. Then he said, "We need to get as many of the team here as possible. I've got a lot to tell you and I don't want to have to keep going over it all."

"It's quite late," said Libby, "and Ma will be coming to get us in soon. And we wouldn't have time to get Max and the dogs over even if they could come."

"Well, as many as we can get here quickly," said Tom.

Sherpa got up. "I can at least get Beelzebub, Leo and Toby." As he shot off down the garden he shouted back, "Don't tell them anything until I get back, will you?"

The five cats settled down to wait, four of them struggling to be patient!

Suddenly they heard Ma calling them. They didn't move, except for Tom, who hid in the bushes. Ma came up the garden to see why the cats weren't coming in. Pa followed her.

"Come on you lot, time to come in."

"Oh, leave them, Ma," said Pa, adding with a noticeable emphasis, "We'll only be gone a couple of hours. They'll be fine and they can get in the house if they want."

Ma sighed, but she was beginning to relax where the cats were concerned, thanks to Pa. "Oh, okay. We'll have to hurry. We're meant to be at Betty and George's by ten to eight."

The two of them walked back down the garden and into the house. A few minutes later they came out again and set off down the drive. Pa laughed and called out, "Be good cats. Bedtime at ten o' clock."

Ma shushed him and then smiled at his apparent joking. The cats knew full well that Pa was actually indicating to them that the kitchen would be free for them to use until ten o' clock!

"Where are they going?" asked Libby.

"I think they're going to something at the church hall," answered Ginny. "Betty rang earlier to ask if they'd go with them. So that they'd know someone, I expect."

Before they could continue their conversation, Sherpa reappeared, followed by Beelzebub, Leo and Toby. Tagging along behind was William, still not quite sure of his place in the group.

Jake got up and said, "Come on down to the kitchen all of you. Ma and Pa have gone out. We've got until ten o' clock."

The animals trooped down to the house and eventually settled in a group on the floor by the kitchen window. By then they were all full of anticipation, waiting to hear what Mangy Tom had to say. Once they had all got comfortable, Jake looked at Mangy Tom and nodded.

The animals sat spellbound for an hour, while Tom recounted his adventures over the past three days. He told them about his encounter with the fox and the young cat -pausing to thank Beelzebub for his 'party trick'! The animals all laughed at that, including Beelzebub, who said, "You're welcome. Glad to have been of use."

However, they were all aware that Tom had put himself in a dangerous situation in order to help the little cat. Jake said, "That was risky. That cat owes you a lot."

Tom grinned secretively. "Actually, I think that you'll find that he more than repaid me!"

Although, at that, the animals looked at him with interest, he continued by describing his meeting with Ginger and the other three yard cats, telling them that it *was* possible that a ringer had been used, and how the stable boy and jockey were likely to be in on the plan.

"What about the trainer?" asked William.

Tom nodded at him. "Good point. The trainer's been in Ireland for a while, looking at new horses."

Beelzebub shook his head. "I still can't see any reason for doing it!" The others nodded. It seemed to be a completely pointless thing to do.

Tom's grin widened. "I think I found out the answer to that as well."

The animals had been listening to him with flattering interest, but their response to this statement was especially satisfying to Tom. For a second or two they sat – mouths open like a group of goldfish – then they started asking him so many questions, none of which he could hear.

Eventually Jake stood up and the hubbub subsided. "Let Tom carry on. He'll explain everything, I'm sure."

Tom nodded his thanks to Jake and went on to describe his second meeting with the young cat, Bertie.

"We had a very interesting conversation about Blue Diamond – his owner's a racing enthusiast – and Bertie told me that Blue Diamond is owned by a very rich sheik, who lives mostly in France. Bertie told me that, firstly, the sheik was planning to come over to see Blue Diamond race at the end of April, a sudden decision. Secondly, someone wanted to buy the mare, but she was too expensive or the sheik wouldn't sell."

Tom looked around at the rest of the team to see if any of them had understood the relevance of these bits of information. However, no-one reacted. They all looked blankly at Tom. Then Sherpa said slowly, "The owner would realise the horse wasn't the right one – that's why it had to go."

The effect on the others was like a series of light bulbs going on. They realised the truth of what Sherpa had said. It made sense of something that had appeared to be completely pointless.

Then Toby said, "What about the man who wanted to buy her? What's he got to do with it?"

Jake had been thinking about that and had begun to have a glimmer of understanding. However, he looked at Mangy Tom, it was his story. "Go on – you tell them."

The animals sat looking impatiently at Tom, who said, "This is only a guess, it might be completely wrong, but this is what I think might have happened. The man offered to buy Blue Diamond, but the sheik wanted too much or wouldn't sell. The man – who's obviously a bit of a crook – hatched a plan. Swop Blue Diamond for a weaker horse, who wouldn't race well – if she didn't look as if she would win the Embury Cup, maybe the sheik would accept a lower offer or agree to sell, whichever was the problem. Then he'd swop the horses back again."

The group were all nodding enthusiastically, realising that Tom had come up with a believable suggestion.

Sherpa said, "Then the owner decided to come over and look at the situation with his horse for himself and that ruined the plan. They had to get rid of the ringer."

Jake stood up again and, when the others were silent, said, "Thanks Tom. That was a major undertaking and you've really brought home the goods."

The others all joined in congratulating Tom, who began to feel quite overcome at all the goodwill and congratulations he was receiving.

Then Toby said, "This man, the one who wanted to buy Blue Diamond, he seems to have been able to get people to do what he wanted."

Tom nodded, "That's why I think he must be a crook. Maybe some big gangster type who has a load of lesser crooks working for him. That jockey was obviously a set up. And the two men who come to the smallholding probably work for him."

"Well, now we've sorted out what's going on," said Sherpa, ever ready for some action, "what are we going to do now?"

That question silenced everyone, since no-one had an answer.

"Can't we see if we can get Pa to help," suggested Leo.

"How?" asked Wesley. They all knew that Pa would be only too willing to deal with the situation, if he knew what was going on. But they were back to the same old problem – communication. Jake was sure Pa knew they were working on a case and had even indicated his willingness to help. It was just so frustrating that they had no idea how to point him in the right direction. They all sat in silence, no-one having any idea how to involve Pa or how to progress with the case themselves. Then Libby spoke up.

"We need to warn Tarran and Max. These men might be dangerous."

"I'll go over tomorrow and tell them," offered Tom.

"I'll come with you," said Sherpa, keen to be doing something. Ginny looked anxiously at him. Sherpa had a tendency to get into dangerous situations without even trying. Jake saw the look and made a sudden decision.

"We'll all go."

The animals first reaction was a shocked silence. Then everyone spoke at once, excited at the prospect of some action.

Wesley said, "But what about Ma?"

"We'll only be a few hours," answered Jake. "She'll be okay when she sees we're back home. Thanks to Pa, she doesn't seem to be so uptight about us being out and about now. How are the rest of you fixed?"

Beelzebub and Leo nodded. William also nodded, but rather slowly. Toby nodded the most enthusiastically of all of them. At last, he had a chance to be in the middle of some action and it would also give him an opportunity to test how well his plan for training Mrs Whittacker was going!

Jake looked at the clock. Ten to ten. "Okay, we'll meet behind the garden wall tomorrow at nine thirty and we'll all go over together." He turned to Tom. "Sorry to ask more of you but could you get Lucy there?"

Tom nodded, "No problem."

Jake then turned to Sherpa. "Could you leave a bit earlier and get Sooty and Patch. We really don't know what's going to happen and I'd like as many of the team there as possible."

"Okay, Boss," said Sherpa, trying to lighten the mood which seemed a bit serious. The others smiled at Sherpa's cheek.

"Okay," continued Jake. "Time now for you visitors to disappear. Ma and Pa will be back in a few minutes." There were brief goodbyes and in thirty seconds only the Dawson's own cats were left in the kitchen.

Just after ten o' clock, Ma and Pa returned. Ma busied herself making a pot of tea, but Pa, who had seen some of the cats and Toby making their way home, knew there had been a meeting. He looked closely at Jake and Jake stared back. Pa knew something was going on and wondered if his help was needed. For the hundredth time both man and cat regretted the problems they had communicating.

CHAPTER TWELVE

The following morning the cats were awake early, feeling a mixture of anticipation and anxiety. They felt they had a good understanding of what had been going on, but they had no idea what would happen next or what they would do about it.

After breakfast, they made their way up to the top of the garden. Before they had left the kitchen, Jake and Pa had exchanged looks and Pa knew something was going on. He wished he knew what it was and if there was any way in which he could help.

All the local members of Spy Club were waiting for Jake and the others behind the garden wall, except Sherpa and Mangy Tom, who had gone on ahead. They set off at a cracking pace, Jake in the lead, and in a very short space of time they reached the edge of Mad Mary's smallholding. They settled in a field out of sight and waited for the others. They were not long in arriving, first Mangy Tom and Lucy and then Sherpa, Sooty, Patch and, to the utter amazement of Jake and the others, Brian! Sherpa grinned, pleased with the effect of his surprise.

"While I was in Garston to fetch Sooty and Patch, I popped along to Brian's to bring him up to date and, as luck would have it, Claire was out."

Brian grinned happily. "Claire left me in the garden, so I used my escape route. She'll be gone for two or three hours so I should be okay."

Although Claire's garden was supposedly dog escape proof, Brian had found a part of the fence which was not secure, and he used it when Claire was not around. The other animals, especially Wesley, were really pleased to see him. Once they had alerted Max and Tarran, the team would be complete.

Mangy Tom skirted the field and made his way to the house where he found Tarran lying outside. When Tarran saw him, he got up and wandered across to him. "Hallo, Mangy Tom, what are you doing here?"

Tom grinned. "Get Max quickly. The whole team is waiting in the field by the stables. We've got news."

Before Tarran could ask any questions, Tom turned and raced back the way he had come. Shortly after, Tarran, now accompanied by Max, followed after him.

When they got to the field, where the rest of the team were waiting, Jake stood up and said, "Right Tom. Can you give us a quick recap of what you told us yesterday for Max and the others."

Mangy Tom, following instructions, repeated the main points to another gawping audience. When he'd finished, the animals all started talking at once, making something of a racket. Jake stood up and gradually there was silence. When everyone was listening, Jake addressed his team.

"We now think we know what's been going on, but we don't really know how we're going to deal with it. We need to speak to Blue Diamond first, now we know it's really her. Right, let's go."

The animals made their way quickly and quietly to Blue Diamond's stable and Lucy took up her position on the water butt. She said something to the rather startled mare. They had a brief conversation, then Lucy turned to the others.

"I've explained to Blue what we think has happened – she's called just Blue – and she said that someone did try to buy her, but her owner told the man that he wanted to run her in the Embury Cup and that she wasn't for sale. She said the man didn't seem very gentlemanly. He got rather bad tempered when her owner refused to sell her."

Then Lucy turned and said something else to the mare, who gave a brief reply.

"I asked her where they took her when she went out in the horsebox and she said she goes out training. Galloping somewhere."

Jake looked at the others and said, "They must be trying to keep her fit."

Before anyone could say anything else, the animals heard a car turning into the yard entrance to the smallholding. Jake turned to Max and Tarran and said, "Stay here. They know you. We'll be nearby."

Max and Tarran settled themselves lying casually in the yard, while the rest of the animals disappeared into the surrounding undergrowth. Lucy stayed put sitting on the water butt, washing her ears and looking completely uninterested in anything going on around her.

The car pulled into the yard and the two men, known to Max and Tarran, got out. They seemed to be rather agitated and had obviously been arguing. They paid no attention to Tarran and the two cats, who seemed to be equally uninterested in them. They went over and stood in front of Blue's stable.

The mare put her ears back and said something that sounded very unflattering.

The taller of the two men, obviously in charge, said, "Go and get the feed and put it in the stable, Charlie."

Charlie looked nervously at the mare and said, "Why me, Frankie? Why don't you do it?"

"Just do as you're told, will you?" responded Frankie snappily. He was obviously not in a good mood. He added, "I need to think what to do."

Charlie looked uneasily at Frankie. "You don't make the decisions. We do what the Fat Controller tells us to do, and you know it."

"I know," Frankie said, harshly. "And I wouldn't let him hear you call him that. He doesn't like being made fun of." He walked up and down in front of Blue's stable obviously very unsettled. "Things are getting out of hand. I don't like it. I think we should get rid of her."

Charlie looked puzzled. "What do you mean?"

"Are you stupid?" said Frankie, then raised his eyebrows theatrically, clearly thinking the answer to that question was a resounding 'yes'. He realised he'd have to spell it out for Charlie to understand. "The whole plan's falling apart and, if we're caught with her, we're the ones that'll cop it not him."

"So what are you suggesting?" asked Charlie, still rather in the dark.

Frankie looked at the mare, who was aware that they were talking about her but, fortunately couldn't understand what they were saying.

"We take her out somewhere isolated and put a bullet in her. We bury her and tell him that she broke a leg out exercising and had to be shot."

The animals, hidden in the undergrowth, listened in horrified disbelief.

"What are we going to do?" whispered Wesley.

"Shush!" Jake was still listening to the two men.

Charlie seemed almost as horrified as Wesley but more for his own safety than the mare's.

"Why do we have to do that? What if we're caught with her body? Can't we just leave her here?"

"If we leave her here, they'll eventually call the police and the woman's seen us. She can identify both of us. We've both got our pictures on police files. If we just tell her we don't want the livery anymore and take the mare away, she won't be suspicious."

Charlie nodded. "Okay, it's up to you. We'll dispose of the mare and then I'm disappearing back to Liverpool. Working for the Fat Controller is too stressful for me! I've had enough."

Jake got up and quietly called his team together but, before he could tell them what he wanted them to do, they noticed Mad Mary standing hidden, at the end of the stable block. She had obviously heard everything the two men had said.

She came forward, eyes blazing, and said furiously, "What are you talking about? If you think I'm going to stand by and let you hurt this mare, you've got another think coming."

Frankie scowled at her and said threateningly, "You'll mind your own business if you know what's good for you."

Mad Mary looked at him for a long searching moment and then said, "I think there's something funny going on here. I'm going to call the police."

As she turned to go, Frankie picked up a long piece of wood leaning against the wall of the stable. Before Mad Mary had fully turned to go, he hit her hard on the side of the head. As she crumpled to the ground, blood pouring from a deep cut on the side of her forehead, the animals stood frozen in shocked horror. Max rushed over to her and rubbed his head comfortingly against her.

Tarran stood absolutely still, staring at Mad Mary; the woman who had taken him in when he had had no home, who had fed him and cared for him and tended his sores and most importantly of all, had loved him unconditionally. He looked at the blood dripping from her head onto the ground and his own blood began to boil. He turned towards Frankie, who had raised the piece of wood once more, obviously intending to hit Mad Mary again and, teeth bared and belly to the floor, he advanced towards Frankie, growling menacingly.

Looking at him there was no doubt that the angry dog was ready to tear the man limb from limb and Frankie, realising he had no chance of getting away if he ran, opened the nearest stable door, which happened to be Blue's, and shut himself inside.

Jake shook himself out of his shocked state and shouted, "Lucy, tell Blue to block the door."

Lucy called out something in French and Blue obligingly moved in front of the stable door, standing looking at the terrified man with her ears back. She had no idea what the men had said about her future, but she knew they had taken her from her home and treated her unkindly. She had also seen them hit the woman who always spoke gently to her and brought her apples and carrots. They were clearly 'no good' and she was happy to help give them their comeuppance. She put her ears back and bared her teeth and Frankie began to realise that his choice of refuge had not been as wise as it could have been!

As soon as the man had shut himself in the stable, Brian had quickly joined Tarran and they stood guard together. Between the two dogs and the mare, Frankie hadn't a chance of getting out of the stable – not in one piece anyway!

Seeing Frankie stuck in the stable, Charlie turned to run and found his way blocked by several hissing cats and a sparky Jack Russell, who ran up to him and started nipping his ankles. He stopped and gave Toby a hefty kick, which sent him flying into the undergrowth. Before Charlie had a chance to do anything, he was set upon by the infuriated cats. In a second Beelzebub was on his back, using his long sharp claws to good effect, so that Charlie screeched in pain. Jake, Sherpa, Leo and Mangy Tom used his legs as a scratching post, while Sooty, Patch and Wesley attacked his ankles.

Seeing that Charlie was being well and truly dealt with, Libby and Ginny went over to Toby, to see if he was alright. The plucky little dog grinned and said he was fine. However, he decided that there were plenty of animals sorting Charlie out, so he sat and watched with a feeling of satisfaction. Charlie collapsed to the floor in an attempt to get Beelzebub off his back. Realising that Beelzebub was doing a good job on his own the other cats backed off and circled the writhing man, hissing and yowling and making a terrible din.

Seeing the animals focussing on Charlie, Frankie made the mistake of trying to get out of the stable. Blue obligingly moved out of his way and he hurriedly opened the door. However, as he went to step outside, he came face to face with two ferocious and angry dogs, who snarled at him with the apparent intention of ripping him to shreds. He quickly stepped back inside the stable, slamming the door behind him. Blue looked at him in amusement as he retreated to the back of the stable again. It was the most fun she'd had for days! She watched Charlie's struggle with equal amusement and felt that, whoever these animals were, they were paying back every grudge she had against the two men.

Seeing that things were under control for the moment, Jake was frantically wondering what they could do to get help when, to his utter amazement and even greater relief, he saw Ma and Pa driving into the house entrance to the smallholding. Why they were there he had no idea, he was just glad to have a human there, whom they could rely on to help.

CHAPTER THIRTEEN

Ma and Pa got out of their car, looking in shock across the yard at the scene outside the stable block. Ma rushed over to her sister and spoke soothingly to her until she was able to sit up. Tarran, feeling that help had arrived, left his watch at the stable door and rushed over to Mad Mary, licking her face and whining.

Pa looked at the man lying on the floor, being guarded by Toby, who was just waiting for an excuse to give him a good bite. Beelzebub had stopped his attack the moment he had seen Pa's car drive into the smallholding and he was now sitting angelically beside Leo. Pa, who had seen Beelzebub in action before, looked at him and raised his eyebrows but, knowing these animals, he realised that whatever had been done had been done for a reason.

Suddenly, Pa noticed Frankie, cowering in the corner of Blue's stable and crossed over towards the door. Blue, to whom he was a stranger, snapped at him and Lucy hurriedly called out, "It's okay Blue, he's one of us. He's a good guy! He's come to help."

Blue looked at Pa and then put her ears forward and bent her head towards him. He put his hand out cautiously to stroke her and noticed some white hairs appearing on her forehead. He touched the area where the blaze had been dyed and a sudden vague comprehension came into his expression. He thought for a minute, remembering his conversation with George, then he shook his head. Without the information the animals had, he was not able to quite get to the truth.

However, he was absolutely certain that something was going on and that, whatever it was, the animals had been investigating it.

Without a word he got out his phone and rang a number.

"Hallo. Could I speak to Detective Inspector Franks, please? It's Roger Dawson of Lower Barton. He knows me."

There was a pause and then Pa spoke again. "Hallo, it's Roger Dawson. I think you should come to my sister-in-law's smallholding in Braybury. It's off the Littlebury Road. I think you'll find two men and a horse you might be interested in. Does the name Blue Diamond mean anything to you?"

There was another pause and then he said, "I honestly don't know, but it's certainly a fishy situation. Especially as they've attacked my sister-in-law." Another pause. "No, I don't think so, but she should receive some medical attention …. Thanks. See you soon."

The animals had listened intently to Pa's conversation with DI Franks and felt that they were now relieved of responsibility. Pa went over to where Ma was using her handkerchief to mop up the blood still dripping from Mad Mary's head and said, "DI Franks is coming and he's going to arrange medical attention for Mary. Is she okay?"

Ma looked at him, fury in her eyes. "He hit her with a piece of wood." She leaned over and patted Tarran. "If it hadn't been for Tarran he might have done worse."

Mad Mary weakly leaned over and put her arm round Tarran. Max looked on approvingly. "Good work, Tarran," he said and Tarran smiled at him.

"I couldn't let him hurt her again. Not after all she's done for me."

And he got another approving nod from Max. Mad Mary turned to the miaowing cat and put her hand on his head. He purred and rubbed against her. Ma looked at Pa, with a puzzled expression on her face. "What exactly is going on?" Then she looked at the animals and said in a bewildered tone of voice, "And why are they all here?"

Before Pa could think of an answer, Mad Mary said weakly, "They were planning to kill the horse. There's something wrong."

Pa nodded. "You're quite right, Mary. If my guess is correct, this horse has been disguised. I've a feeling there's a white blaze hidden under some brown dye. Anyway," he turned to Ma, "see if you can get Mary inside and I'll wait for the police."

Ma helped Mad Mary to her feet and slowly walked her back to the house, followed anxiously by Max and Tarran.

Pa looked at Jake and said, "I imagine this has something to do with the racehorse George was telling me about."

Jake looked steadily at Pa, a sign that he was on the right track, but Charlie, naturally thinking the remark had been made to him, and not to a load of cats and dogs, said bitterly, "I knew it was a bad idea."

Jake continued to look at Pa, who realised he was wondering what Ma and Pa were doing at the smallholding.

Pa grinned. "When you all disappeared, I knew something was going on. Then Ma noticed you were gone and was convinced that you'd come over here. She insisted we came to see. Fortunately, as it happens."

By now Charlie was looking at Pa as if he was completely insane. Pa looked back at him, with barely concealed anger. "Was it you who attacked my sister-in-law?"

Charlie immediately forgot Pa's conversation with the animals and pointed at the stable, where Frankie was still hiding, hoping not to be noticed. Charlie started to get up, but Toby growled threateningly and Brian, realising that Frankie was safely penned in the stable by Blue, went over to join him. Charlie shrank back on the ground again. Whenever he looked like moving, the two dogs bared their teeth and growled.

Pa looked thoughtfully at Brian, who was certainly showing a side of his nature that Pa had not only never seen but didn't realise existed. He smiled at the big dog and said, "I don't suppose Claire knows you're here, does she? Ma said she was going out, so I suppose you took your chance."

Brian looked at him and Pa was sure that he was grinning. "I'd go home now if I was you. Before you're missed."

Brian obediently got up and, with a word of farewell to the others, set off back home. Jake called after him. "Thanks Brian, you were great. See you." Brian looked back, smiling gratefully. He still tended to worry that he wouldn't do things right and praise always made him feel better. He called out, "Thanks." Then he headed happily off towards Garston.

Seeing that everything seemed to be under control, Sooty and Patch said their goodbyes and followed after Brian. No sooner had they gone than a police car turned into the yard, followed by a paramedic ambulance.

DI Franks got out of the police car, followed by a police constable, PC Watkins, also known to Pa and the animals. A paramedic got out of the ambulance and approached Pa, who directed him to the house.

PC Watkins stood by the car, while DI Franks walked over to the group by the stables. He looked hard at the animals sitting quietly watching him. The last time he had dealt with a case involving Pa, he had been surrounded by animals. The same animals!

When he reached the stables, DI Franks looked down at the man on the floor, who was clutching his bleeding head. He had twice before seen men with injuries like that. He looked questioningly at Pa and said, "Which one of them does that?"

Pa looked round at the cats but, feeling that everything was now in safe hands, Beelzebub and Leo had also slipped off home. Pa looked back at DI Franks and said, in an expressionless tone of voice, "The vicar's cat."

DI Franks looked at him with a startled expression on his face, not sure if Pa was having him on. Then he sighed, thinking that he would never understand so he might as well not try, shook his head and got on with the job in hand.

"Why did you phone me?" he asked Pa. "Can you explain what you think is going on?"

Pa looked at him and grinned. "No, I don't think I can," he replied to the DI's surprise. "I'm not really sure myself what's going on. I just know something's not right and I think it's to do with that mare in the stable. And, anyway, these men attacked my sister-in-law."

He went on to explain what had brought them to the smallholding and the scene he and Ma had discovered when they got there.

"You need to speak to my sister-in-law, Mary. I think she can tell you more of what's been going on."

DI Franks nodded and then called across to PC Watkins, "Call for back up, Watkins. We need to get these two down to the station. Even if nothing else is going on, they're guilty of assault."

PC Watkins got back in the car and, in a very short space of time, two squad cars arrived at the smallholding.

Meanwhile, Mad Mary had been brought outside by Ma and the paramedic, who wanted her checked out at the hospital as she had a head injury. DI Franks told her he would call at the hospital to speak to her and then the paramedic drove both women to Littlebury Hospital, Ma refusing to leave her sister on her own.

As they watched the ambulance drive out of the yard, Pa began to explain to the DI what he knew about Blue Diamond, who was watching them suspiciously from her stable, while still managing to keep an eye on the terrified Frankie. Puzzled at what Pa was telling him, DI Franks said, "But the racehorse was only stolen on Saturday night. You say this mare has been here for a fortnight."

Pa admitted that this was so, but insisted that he believed that, somehow, the mare they were looking at was Blue Diamond. The animals all watched, frustrated that they couldn't tell Pa and the DI how it had been done. DI Franks had met Pa before though and, other than his habit of surrounding himself with animals, had found him down to earth and not given to imagining things. Therefore, he was inclined to believe him although he, too, could think of no way in which it could have happened. He knew he should go over and have a look to see if the mare had any sign of a blaze on her forehead but one look at her had convinced him that it might not be a good idea.

When the two squad cars arrived, the DI formally arrested the two men, for assault to begin with, and they were taken off in the squad cars. Fortunately, a word from Lucy meant that Blue happily stood back for the police to get Frankie, who was almost relieved to be arrested if it meant being able to get away from Blue and the dogs.

Once the two cars had left, DI Franks turned to look at the mare and said to Pa, "What do we do with her?"

Pa smiled. "I'll feed her and she'll be fine for now. She's been here quite happily for the past fortnight. If Mary's not back tonight, I'll come over to see to her. I imagine once we've established that she really is Blue Diamond, someone from the yard where she's trained will come and fetch her. If I were you, I'd contact them and get someone to come over and identify her today."

DI Franks nodded. "I'll get on to it."

He shook Pa's hand and thanked him, and then he and PC Watkins got in their car and drove back to Littlebury Police Station.

After they had left, he fed Blue, who was quite friendly towards him, having decided that he was, in Lucy's words, 'a good guy'! Then he fed the chickens, which was what Mad Mary had been coming out to do when she had heard the two men talking. Having sorted out the yard, he walked over to the house, fetched Max and Tarran and then locked up.

He walked over to the boot of his car and opened it up, calling out to the animals, "Nonstop to Lower Barton." He stood back while the animals all piled into the car. It was a bit of a squeeze, but the animals were glad not to have to make the return journey on foot.

Pa looked across at Lucy, who was still sitting on the water butt. As he watched, she jumped down and set off across the fields, closely followed by Mangy Tom, making sure she was going in the right direction. Having watched the two cats cross the field and disappear, Pa got in the car and set off towards Lower Barton. Although some things were still not clear and there seemed to be a lot of questions still to be answered, it looked as though Spy Club's latest investigation was coming to a successful end.

CHAPTER FOURTEEN

When Pa got home with his load of passengers, he opened the back door and left it open so the animals, cats and dogs, could come and go as they pleased. Toby and William, feeling they had been away from their homes for long enough, set off home, rather reluctantly in Toby's case, although he was beginning to feel the effects of Charlie's kick. Before they left Jake thanked them both for their help and said he'd be in touch.

The rest of the animals settled in the kitchen to discuss the events of the morning. All of them expressed relief at Pa's timely arrival, without which they would have found it difficult to resolve the situation. They all found it mildly amusing that Ma, who had no idea what the animals did and wouldn't believe it if she was told, was the one responsible for getting Pa to the right place at the right time.

After lunch, which Pa ate in the kitchen, Ma rang to say that Mad Mary was being allowed home and could he come and fetch them? Ma also wanted him to bring her a bag with some clothes and night things as she planned to stay with her sister for a few days. Half an hour later, overnight bag in hand, Pa left for the hospital, taking Max and Tarran with him.

Jake and the remaining cats settled down, feeling rather tired after the exciting events of the morning. They were asleep on their beds by the kitchen window when Pa got back. He sat at the kitchen table and watched the cats who were gradually waking up.

"Well, you lot," he said, "I've got news."

The cats immediately sat up, alert and anxious to hear what Pa had to tell them. With no-one else in the house to worry about, Pa was able to talk freely to the cats, and had got to the stage where it didn't even feel odd anymore!

While the cats sat in silence watching him, Pa told them what he had found out from DI Franks, who had been at the hospital to speak to Mad Mary when Pa arrived. The DI had already questioned Charlie and Frankie and had just about sorted out what had been going on.

Afraid of what the 'Fat Controller' might do to him and determined not to incriminate himself, Frankie had refused to say anything. However, this had turned out not to matter, as Charlie had talked enough for both of them, implicating not just the two of them but everyone involved in the plot to steal Blue Diamond, including the 'Fat Controller'! It seemed that Mangy Tom had been right in all his suggestions, including the fact that the man behind it was a wealthy London businessman, who tended to resort to criminal acts when he was displeased! He was about to become very displeased as the London CID were on their way to arrest him!

Pa looked at the animals and said, "But I expect you already knew all that, didn't you?"

A long, hard stare from Jake told him that he was right. Then Pa voiced what they were all thinking.

"It's a pity you couldn't tell me what was going on. I'm sure you'd worked it all out ages ago. Still, as usual, we got there."

Jake rubbed up against Pa's leg to show he agreed. Pa leant down to stroke his head. "You've a fine team there. Just take care, all of you."

"Try telling that to Sherpa," called out Wesley cheekily. Sherpa gave him a gentle cuff round the ear and all the cats laughed. Hearing the mews and yips coming from the group Pa laughed, although he had no idea why!

He went over to put the kettle on and, as he made himself a cup of tea, he gave the cats the rest of his news. DI Franks had told him that they had been in touch with the Orchard Racing Stables, who had sent someone over to the smallholding. They had confirmed that the mare was Blue Diamond, as a result of which the mare's owner was flying over from France and would be coming with someone from the stables to collect the mare the next day. Pa was planning to ask George if he wanted to go over to see the mare before she left.

Pa didn't manage to get any further as all this information set the cats talking excitedly amongst themselves and the kitchen was filled with miaows and yowls for the next few minutes.

However, Pa's next words successfully silenced them from sheer shock. He held a hand up for quiet and then said, "Do you all want to come?"

The cats could hardly believe what they were hearing. Pa was actually offering to arrange for all of Spy Club to be there when Blue's owner collected her! Jake went over to rub round Pa's legs again, his way of saying, "Yes please." The other cats couldn't resist joining him, and Pa found himself surrounded by purring cats. Showing how much he now knew of Spy Club, Pa looked at Sherpa and said, "Make sure everyone's here at nine 'o' clock tomorrow morning."

Sherpa, grinning from ear to ear, promptly got up and left to spread the word, delighted to be the one to tell the others the good news. As luck would have it, he also saw Mangy Tom, who said he would arrange for Lucy, Sooty and Patch to be there. Pa got on the phone and extended his invitation to George, whose excitement was clear even though the cats couldn't hear what he was saying.

Pa then took his cup of tea and went through to the snug, leaving the cats to talk excitedly about the following morning's adventure.

CHAPTER FIFTEEN

At a quarter to nine the next morning, the Lower Barton members of Spy Club were waiting in the garden but, to their alarm, there was no sign of Pa or the four by four. Surely he hadn't gone without them. None of the Dawson cats had heard him leaving and didn't know where he could have gone.

Then they heard the car pulling into the drive and rushed to meet it. In the back, grinning from ear to ear, was Brian! Pa looked at the other animals.

"Thought I'd give Claire the chance to get out and about without having a dog to worry about!" he said and winked at the animals.

He opened the boot of the vehicle and the animals all piled in to join Brian. They managed to arrange themselves so that no-one ended up with a paw in their eye and then talked excitedly all the way to Mad Mary's smallholding. Fortunately, Pa didn't seem to mind the racket although George, who arrived just as Pa was shutting the boot, looked at the crowd of animals in amazement, especially when he saw William crouched between Brian's front paws. He had to resist the temptation to put his hands over his ears during the short journey.

Pa simply said, "They were there when the men were caught. I thought they'd enjoy a trip out."

George, full of anticipation, simply nodded in agreement, not having the faintest idea what Pa was going on about! It made no difference to him. He was going to see Blue Diamond and that was all that concerned him. Pa could have had a car full of pink elephants and he would have accepted it!

When they got to the smallholding, Ma and Mad Mary were in the stable yard with Max and Tarran, who were expecting them all as Mangy Tom and the other three cats had already arrived and were sitting in the field. The six watched from their various places as the remaining members of Spy Club all streamed out of the car boot.

Ma looked at the crowd of cats and dogs piling out of the car and opened her mouth to speak. Before she could say anything, Pa said, "They were hanging about, so I thought I'd bring them over." He smiled at Ma, who had become utterly speechless – a very unusual condition for her.

Before she could recover her power of speech, they heard a car turning into the yard entrance. Everyone was struck dumb, not just Ma, when a very sleek, very expensive chauffeur driven limousine appeared.

When it stopped the chauffeur got out, respectfully opened the back door and waited. A tall expensively dressed man got out and, with a word of thanks to the chauffeur, made his way across the yard to where the four humans were standing waiting.

The man, speaking with a slight accent, said, "Is one of you two gentlemen Roger Dawson?"

Pa stepped forward. "I'm Roger Dawson."

The man held out his hand to Pa, as he introduced himself. Pa shook his hand and introduced Ma, Mad Mary and George. The man shook hands with the three of them, but they said nothing, struck dumb by the man's appearance. Unlike the animals, they had not been aware that Blue's owner was a wealthy sheik.

The man looked across at the mare, staring eagerly out of her stable door at her owner. Her blaze was clear to see and her coat was shining, thanks to the efforts of Ma and Mad Mary.

The man looked back at the four humans and said, "I am Blue Diamond's owner and I believe I owe you a debt of gratitude." He looked at Mad Mary, a large plaster across the side of her head, and added, "Especially you, madam. I understand you received that injury defending my lovely Blue."

Mad Mary, remembering the two men who were planning to kill the mare, forgot her nerves and said, "They were talking about killing her. What else could I do?"

The man smiled and nodded. "You will be very wary of taking another livery after your experiences lately."

Mad Mary looked determined. "There won't be any more, I can assure you!"

"You will keep your faithful old Land Rover then?" said the man.

Ma, Pa and Mad Mary all looked at him in surprise.

"You and DI Franks had a good chat then?" Pa wondered how much DI Franks had actually told the man.

The man laughed and looked round at all the animals sitting quietly, listening. "According to DI Franks, these animals played their part too." He turned to Mad Mary. "Do they all belong to you?"

She shook her head. "Some are my sister and brother-in-law's, some live in Lower Barton and some I've never seen before!"

The man laughed and said, jokingly, "Perhaps they're in a gang."

The others all laughed, Pa more than any of them. Then he said to the man, "I assume you're here to collect Blue Diamond."

The man nodded. "A horsebox from Oakland Stables should be here any time now, but I wanted the chance to see you all and thank you first."

He obviously wondered where George fitted in and Pa turned to him and said, "George is a newcomer to our village. He's been following Blue Diamond's progress since she first started racing and is looking forward to seeing her run in the Embury Cup. He says she's bound to win."

The man laughed. "I hope so." Then he gestured to George and said, "Come and meet her."

The two men made their way across to the stable and were soon deep in a discussion about Blue's finer points. By the look on George's face, he'd just been given a glimpse of Heaven.

Ma was just about to suggest a cup of tea, when they heard the sound of a lorry turning into the entrance to the smallholding. They all watched as a gleaming horsebox pulled into the yard, driven by the yard manager and accompanied by a stable boy and Blue Diamond's trainer, newly back from Ireland.

Mangy Tom, watching the box pull up, looked on in amazement. Sitting on the stable boy's lap, large as life and grinning from ear to ear was –

"Ginger!" Tom's amazed exclamation made all the animals look, in equal amazement, at the newcomer, who had leapt out of the horsebox as soon as the door had opened.

He strolled casually over to the group of animals, still grinning, and said, "This is Spy Club, I suppose. I was hoping some of you would be here."

Mangy Tom nodded. "How did you manage to get them to bring you?"

Ginger shrugged. "I got in the horsebox and wouldn't get out. I've been in it before, so they weren't too bothered."

Mangy Tom nodded to the patch of grass opposite the stables. "Come on everyone, let's go over here, out of the way."

All the animals made their way to the grass and settled down with Mangy Tom and Ginger in the middle. After a brief glance to check that there wasn't going to be any trouble between Ginger and the others, the humans gave their attention to the mare. All except Pa, who looked closely at the two cats and thought that they seemed to know each other. "I wonder how?" he thought. It occurred to him, remembering the night a clearly anxious Libby had brought him for some food, that the stray might well have taken his investigations to the racing stables, and he marvelled again at the resourcefulness of the team.

Meanwhile the men from the stables were making a fuss of Blue, who was thrilled to be back with the people who cared for her. She found time to say something to Lucy and then turned back to enjoy the human attention.

Ginger turned to Lucy as she joined the rest of the team. He looked appreciatively at the pretty longhaired tortoiseshell and said, "You the one who speaks French?" Lucy nodded. "Hm," continued Ginger. "Beauty and Brains." and Lucy giggled. Then she looked at the others and gave them Blue's message. "Blue said to say thank you for your help."

Then Mangy Tom introduced Ginger to the others, and they all settled down and listened while Tom told Ginger of his meeting with Bertie on the way home and Ginger told them all about the disappearance of the stable boy and jockey, of whom there was still no sign.

"They'll be caught eventually," said Ginger. "The word's gone round racing stables across the country and probably further. If they try to get a job in any yard, they'll be nabbed."

Then Ginger wanted to know all about Spy Club. Everyone talked at once, eager to tell the visitor all about their adventures, and Ginger couldn't understand a word. Eventually Jake stood up and the animals fell silent. Every member of the team was given the chance to talk about their own part in the investigations and, by the time they'd finished, it was clear that Ginger would have loved to become a member.

While the animals had been talking, Blue Diamond had been readied for her journey back to the racing stables. Eventually the stable boy, watched closely by her owner and trainer, led her carefully up the ramp of the horsebox.

"What's 'goodbye' in French?" Jake asked Lucy.

"Au revoir," she answered.

And a chorus of 'ow revor, Blue Diamond," echoed across the yard, much to the amusement of the humans, although they had no idea what the noise was all about. Blue Diamond turned to give them all one last look and nodded her head, before disappearing into the horsebox.

Ten minutes later the horsebox was ready to go. The stable boy called to Ginger, who said a regretful goodbye to the Spy Club members and promised to send Mangy Tom's best wishes to the other stable cats. Then he jumped into the front of the horsebox and, a couple of minutes later, the box pulled out of the yard on its way back to Oakland.

The mare's owner turned to the four humans and thanked them once again. He then told them he would arrange for them all, including Betty, to be his guests at the racecourse, when Blue Diamond raced in the Embury Cup. They would be able to go down into the paddock before the race, after having lunch in his private box. They were all thrilled, especially George of course, although the others knew they could expect to have a wonderful day. George couldn't wait to get home and tell Betty they were going to be guests of a sheik.

The man then said 'goodbye' to them all, smiled and waved a hand in the direction of the group of animals, and was driven off in the limousine, almost certainly to be awaiting Blue Diamond when she reached the Oakland Stables.

CHAPTER SIXTEEN

Left alone in the yard, the four humans stood about, not really sure what to do next. The past couple of hours had been something of a whirlwind.

Eventually, Ma said, "Come on, I'll make us all a nice cup of tea."

As one, Jake, Libby, Ginny and Wesley immediately looked at Toby, daring him to say anything. They were all remembering the comment he had once made about Ma's tendency to make a 'nice cup of tea' at every available opportunity. Toby looked back at them, the picture of innocence.

"What?" he said, trying not to grin.

The humans turned towards the house and then Pa remembered the rather large group of animals, sitting waiting. He paused, looking uncertainly at them. Mad Mary just smiled. "Let them come in. I don't know what they're all doing here, or what they were doing here yesterday but I'm glad they were. They certainly sorted that nasty pair of crooks out. Anyway, they seem happy enough together so they're unlikely to have a dust up and break all the china!"

The animals needed no second invitation and, led by Max and Tarran, followed the humans into the house. George, finally back on planet Earth, watched them curiously and said, "Why *are* they here?"

For once, Pa didn't have to think of an answer. Ma sighed theatrically and said, "Don't ask, George. Just don't ask!"

Fortunately, Mad Mary's kitchen was large and had a big cooking range on one side. The animals made their way across to the range and settled together to enjoy its warmth and to chat quietly together.

After Ma had made the tea, the humans settled at the kitchen table, a large plate of Mad Mary's delicious homemade biscuits in the middle, and also chatted. The chat, of course, with both humans and animals was about the events of the past few days, although the animals through their investigations, had a better knowledge of events than the humans.

Jake thanked his team for their various efforts, especially Mangy Tom and Lucy. The whole team felt a good deal of satisfaction. It had been a difficult investigation, but they had triumphed yet again. Pa looked across at the group and nodded slightly. The animals all stared back and then Jake returned the nod.

After the humans had finished their tea, Pa stood up and said he and George and the visiting animals needed to get going. Ma was staying on with Mad Mary for another couple of days.

However, before Pa had a chance to move, they heard a noise outside. A large vehicle had stopped in the house entrance to the smallholding. Everyone, humans and animals, got up to go out and see what was going on.

When they reached the house yard, they gazed in dumbstruck awe at the sight of a transporter lorry, on the top of which was a brand new, top of the range, black Land Rover!

The driver came across and said, "Miss Mary Morton?"

Mad Mary weakly held up her hand and the man asked, "Where do you want me to put it?"

Mad Mary opened and shut her mouth and then managed to say, in a faint voice, "It's not mine. I didn't order it."

The man handed her an expensive looking envelope with her name on it. With shaking hands, she opened it, while Ma and Pa cheekily looked over her shoulder. She opened a sheet of equally expensive notepaper, but her hands were shaking so much that she couldn't read what was written on the paper. She gave the note to Pa and said, "You read it."

Pa, glad that the animals could hear as well, read loudly and clearly.

Dear Miss Morton,

Please accept this small gift as a token of my appreciation of your care for Blue Diamond. I believe she owes her life, in part, to you.

I look forward to watching her win the Embury Cup in the company of you and your family.

Sincerely,

"I can't read the name," said Pa. "It's a scrawl."

Everyone looked at the very expensive vehicle, which the deliveryman was untying. Jake nudged Max and whispered, "You won't want to know us, now you'll be whizzing about in that!"

Max looked at Jake and smiled. "Hardly whizzing. You know Mad Mary never drives faster than twenty miles an hour. She'll probably drive extra carefully in this, afraid to damage it."

"I can't accept that!" Mad Mary was saying. "I didn't do anything."

Pa was about to speak when Ma got in first. "To begin with, you didn't get that crack on the head by doing nothing, and secondly, you don't refuse a present from a sheik. They get very offended if you do. You'll write him a nice thankyou note and enjoy the looks on everyone's faces, when you turn up in *that*!" She smiled, good humouredly. "Puts my new car in the shade."

The four humans laughed although, secretly, Pa couldn't help thinking that it was a pity the animals didn't get their share of the thanks. He decided that he would find a way to reward them all.

They all watched as the man got the car off the transporter and parked it in front of the house. He gave two sets of keys to Mad Mary and left, with a generous tip from Pa in his pocket. In spite of the others urging her to have a go in her new car, she refused because she said that she felt too shaky.

"I'll bring Ma home in it on Sunday," she promised.

Then Pa gathered up the animals going back to Lower Barton, including Brian. Sooty and Patch sneaked in as well, wanting to stay with the team a bit longer. It was rather a squash, but nobody minded.

Mangy Tom stayed, feeling that he needed to check Lucy got home safely. He would return to Ma and Pa's as soon as he was sure she'd be okay. He tried to imagine her making her way to the racing stables and back and came to the conclusion that she'd probably end up in Glasgow!

Pa dropped George off before going home. George managed a heartfelt thank you, before charging into the house to tell an amused Betty all about it.

Smiling at George's enthusiasm, Pa drove home only to find that he couldn't get into the drive, which was covered with large cardboard boxes. He parked on the road, then got out of the car and let the animals out.

Together they approached the boxes, which turned out to have come from a very exclusive pet supplies company. Several of the boxes contained cat and dog food and treats, and others a large variety of luxurious pet beds.

An envelope, addressed to Pa, was taped to the top box. He opened it and read the contents to the animals.

Dear Mr Dawson,

As you know, I am well aware that the group of animals I saw at your sister-in-law's yard played an important role in safeguarding Blue Diamond and bringing about the arrest of the two men who stole her.

I leave it to you to distribute the contents of the boxes in an appropriate way.

Many Thanks,

Again, Pa couldn't read the scrawled signature.

"Well," he said to the animals. "At last you get some recognition for your efforts. I'll go through the boxes and sort out a fair division of the contents, although I can't think how I'm going to explain it to your owners."

The animals were giving the pile of boxes the once over, smelling the good things inside. There was one packet lying next to where the letter had been taped. Pa picked it up and looked at it closely for a few seconds. Then he turned to Beelzebub and said thoughtfully, "This one's addressed to you."

Clearly written on the parcel were the words – For The Vicar's Cat.

Pa saw all the animals watching him, so he opened the parcel carefully. When he saw what was inside, he began laughing helplessly. As each animal saw the item, they all joined in, until everyone was rolling round, weak with laughter, including Beelzebub. The sheik clearly had a sense of humour.

Inside the packet was an extra-large, extra-strong, top of the range cat scratcher!

Milton Keynes UK
Ingram Content Group UK Ltd.
UKHW030619110824
446752UK00004B/50